Bianca has woven a beautiful love story set in the Australian outback. Her attention to detail is excellent and she has captured exactly how folks live and work on a cattle property. I thoroughly enjoyed reading it and I look forward to many more stories written by this author.
~ Rita-Marie Lenton
Author and Celebrant

I couldn't put the book down! The storyline was a beautifully written account of finding love in outback Australia. I loved how thoroughly detailed the chapters were, and how much research had gone into ensuring certain aspects were factually accurate.
~ Casey Bahara
Graphic Designer

Love After

Dutchman's Road

BIANCA TODD

Love After Dutchman's Road
Copyright © 2024 Bianca Todd
First published 2024

Disruptive Publishing
17 Spencer Avenue
Deception Bay QLD 4508
Australia
disruptivepublishing.com.au

Book cover design: Fay Kennedy and Disruptive Publishing
Front cover image: Casey Bahara

ISBN: 978-1-7636156-1-8 Print
ISBN: 978-1-7636156-2-5 eBook

Dedicated to all the hardworking

farming communities

..:. and to all the romantics

DISCLAIMER

Love After Dutchman's Road is a work of fiction.

All the names, characters, places, businesses, incidents, and events in this book are the product of the author's imagination.

Any resemblance to actual persons, living or dead, or actual events is purely coincidental.

CONTENT WARNING

This book includes elements that may not be suitable for some readers:

- violence
- trauma
- mental health issues

Readers who may be sensitive to these issues should take note.

CHAPTER ONE

It was late May, almost wintertime in the western town of Chilly, a remote country town at the foot of a mountain range in the central interior of the state. The next town, Huntsville, was about fifty kilometres away, and the closest big town, Braham, was over two hundred kilometres away in the opposite direction.

Like many little country towns, Chilly has a wide main street, the shops have old-fashioned front facades—some of them weathered—that look like they have been there many years. There is a church, a post office, a school, a hotel, a motel, a grocery store, and other assorted little stores. Chilly has a community hall where many a dance or party has been held to celebrate an occasion. There's also a small hospital, a police station, a produce store, and other farm supply businesses.

The Douglas family were one of the original farmers to settle in the area back in the old days when there were no cars, tractors, or general stores. Farming back then was challenging work, all done by hand, and surviving on the land meant a hard life.

Bree is a sixth-generation farmer and she is proud of her family farm, *The Flats*. She has two older brothers, but they want nothing to do with the farm, they hardly come out to visit their parents, Paul and Beth. Bree's oldest brother, William, and his wife Janice and their three children, live interstate and never contact Paul and Beth. Her older brother, Jeff, lives interstate as well, but in a different state to William. Jeff is married to Netty, and they do not have any children.

Bree works at the produce store three days a week, as well as running the family farm; many of the customers are other farmers or workers on nearby properties.

She had finished her shifts at the produce store for the week, and said bye to Phil, the owner. As she rounded the corner of the building she stopped and looked at her pride and joy: her black Landcruiser ute, 'BB' (for 'Black Beauty') fitted with a bullbar, spotlights, UHF (Ultra High Frequency radio) aerial and her new 4 x 4 tyres.

'BB sits up a bit high with the new tyres,' she thought. *'If I get time on the weekend I'll give BB a wash, she's looking dirty.'* There are no drive-through car washes in Chilly, water is a precious item, especially on the farms.

Bree is twenty-five years old, and she will turn twenty-six in early December. She was seventeen years old when she left school in year eleven to run the family farm after her dad, Paul, had a heart attack. Because of his heart condition, Paul could not work the farm anymore, even gardening made him tired. It meant that life for Bree had changed: from wanting to go to university to study to become a veterinarian to now running the family farm. She didn't mind that she did not get to go to university, as she loved the farm and the outdoors. She was a farm girl through-and-through. Life also changed for Paul: from being a hardworking farmer to being a man now unable to do much at all. It was sad to see, and Paul had his 'bad' days when he was angry at not being able to do anything.

Bree's mum, Beth, ran the house, she was a great cook and made sure everyone was fed and taken care of. Beth tried her best with Paul, and she could see how hard it was for him. But their love — their marriage — was something Bree hoped to have one day herself, as their love had withstood so much during the many years they had been together.

'Oh well, I better get moving,' thought Bree, *'first call into the local shop to get some chips and nibblies for tonight'.* "Hi Bree, how are you … got the munchies have you?" asked Ruth, the owner of the store. Bree knew Ruth from her mum's CWA branch.

"No, Ruth, having a get-together with the boys tonight," she replied. Now to the pub to get a carton of beer, which would be her share for tonight. "Hi, Johnno, a carton of beer and a bag of ice please," Bree asked.

Johnno replied, "So where is the party tonight, and am I invited?" With that she gave a laugh, the cheeky bugger, Johnno, was friendly and always joked around. His wife Terry would have given him a look if she were there.

Oh well, she had to get going. Bree couldn't wait for tonight, as the week had been so busy and she needed to unwind. Driving home she was thinking about what she must do when she got there. The music was loud in her ute, thanks to a good stereo system, and she was singing along with her favourite country music songs.

Home at last, time to start setting everything up. She got the Esky and grabbed the ice out of her ute, put the beer in the esky and then poured the bag of ice over the beer. Next, it was out to set up the fire pit; even though there were no fire bans, she insisted that any fire be in a pit. She had too much to lose if a fire started. "Okay, let's set up the fire pit, and chop some firewood," said Bree to herself.

As Bree was chopping the firewood, she thought it wouldn't hurt to take an armful inside to her mum. She didn't know how much there was inside, and with a cold front coming firewood was going to be needed to heat the house up.

Bree had a list of jobs she needed to do tomorrow, so even though she wanted to let her hair down and relax tonight, she had to remember to watch how much alcohol she drank. Oh, and she must remember to grab a bottle of water to drink as well. She had to move cattle tomorrow, so she needed to be sharp and know what she was doing.

After much work she had everything set up for the night. With the fire pit and firewood done, and the drinks in the Esky, she picked up a big armful of firewood and took it inside for her mum, Beth. Then Bree went back outside to tie up three of the four dogs they had on the farm. Most of them were working dogs, but Risso was Paul's favourite dog, and as Risso was getting on in years he did not work on the farm anymore. He was a house dog now, so Risso spent his days sitting beside Paul, or if he was asleep on the lounge, Risso was laying at his feet.

Next, Bree was into the freezer to dig out the five pizzas for tonight, and then into the shower. Because the cold front was coming through—which meant it was going to get really cold outside—Bree dug out her thick coat and beanie. She put on her usual jeans and shirt and a jumper and socks, and then grabbed her coat and beanie and went out to the kitchen.

Bree had a few girlfriends, but they were into dresses and getting their nails done. The girly things. That was *not* her! She was friendly with all the blokes' girlfriends, but she was not close with any of them, except for Olivia. Olivia had never let Bree down.

Owing to her brothers not wanting anything to do

with the farm—even when they were younger—Bree would be out helping her dad and working alongside him. Some days she did not want to go to school, she just wanted to work on the farm. She was more a bloke than a girl, she didn't do girly things, and was much more likely to 'get in and do' what the blokes did. Most of the time she was in jeans and a shirt and boots, only rarely—and it was rarely—did Bree wear a dress and have makeup on and her hair done. It was only on special occasions that this happened, and it had not happened now for a long time.

Bree had been hurt in the past when someone said something about her that was untrue. It was incorrect, but it soon became gossip. She had gone to school with most of the girls in Chilly, so she knew what they were like. In a small town gossip gets around real fast, you only have to tell one person, and next minute the whole town knows. That was why she now kept to herself; she knew the hurt from being a victim of gossip. Even though it was over a year ago, Bree was careful not to be the subject of town gossip again.

Hearing a musical car horn, she knew her best mate, Cody, had arrived. Bree and Cody, and all the other blokes, had known each other for many years. Well, that is how a small country town operates, everyone knows everyone. Cody was always early, and he was loved by the Douglas family. He was nearly twenty-six years of age, a year older than Bree, and come late December he would turn twenty-seven. In the Patrick family Cody was the only one not married. He had three older brothers who were all married with children. His younger sister was married to a farmer in the Chilly area, but he did not see much of her.

The Patrick family owned a large property, called *Aurora Station,* and ran sheep and cattle, and grew wheat on it as well. The Patricks were well known and respected throughout the area, and had been in Chilly the same amount of time as Bree's family. The head of the family was Cody's father, Thomas, and sadly Cody's mother, Annabelle, had died five years earlier after a long illness. Paul and Beth had always treated Cody like a son, but even more so after Annabelle passed away.

Cody knocked on the back door and was welcomed by a big hug from Bree's mum.

"Cody, son, come in and have a coffee," Beth said. "Thanks, Mum. White with three sugars, please," he replied.

Cody went to the verandah and sat down and said hi to Paul. They spoke about the weather and the price of cattle, and Cody asked if there was anything he could help with on the farm.

"How are you at riding a horse?" Paul asked. The newly bought cows — which were pregnant when they got them — were close to giving birth. "Bree has to move the pregnant cows down to the yard near the shed tomorrow, she could use a hand. Just wish I could get out of the bloody chair and help her. She does so much around here."

Cody replied that he would help Bree, and that Paul had to stop worrying; he was always here to help them. As he said it, Cody reached out and touched Paul's arm in reassurance.

Beth arrived with Cody's coffee, "Cody love, you need to cut out the sugar in your coffee, you know it's no good for you."

"Okay, Mum, I will try," he said, grinning. Beth cared for all Bree's friends like they were her own.

Cody turned to Paul and said, "What has happened, has happened, and you have to learn to deal with it. Getting angry all the time doesn't help you, and you know what the specialist said: no stress!"

"Well, the specialist is not a farmer, farming is a very stressful job," replied Paul.

Paul knew Cody was right, too much stress and he may not see another sunrise. "You give me enough stress," said Beth, "when you go on about not being able to do things. We went through all this months ago with the specialist. You give me so much grief, that's why I'm so grey."

Bree came out to the kitchen and made a coffee; she knew that Cody had arrived, and that he would be talking to her dad.

As Bree joined them on the verandah, Paul said hello

to her, and wanted to know if she had everything ready for tonight. "Dad, please stop worrying," Bree said, " I have everything sorted for tonight. Oh, we are going to need more firewood as well, so I will head out tomorrow with the boys and get a couple of loads. The weather report said there is a cold front coming through, and we can expect frosts and strong westerly winds with it."

Paul said, "You be careful using the chainsaw and the axe, I just sharpened them yesterday." He could do small jobs like that, but he had to make sure he did not overdo it. Even though he did light tasks, like sharpening the axe, it still tired him out quickly. Paul always worried about Bree operating machinery or chainsaws or using an axe. Even though she was very capable he still worried.

Bree thought, *'Why is it that he cannot trust me like he would trust a bloke? Just because I am a woman it doesn't mean I can't do the same things.'* She was definite that she was not going to be tied to the stove or the house. That was not who she was. Yes, she was quite capable of running a house, cooking, and cleaning, etc., but she was not a homebody: outside running the farm — that was her.

Cody spoke up, "Paul, please don't worry, I'll help Bree do everything and we'll organise the boys to get firewood for you."

"Bloody stupid heart, I feel like I'm an invalid and a

problem to you all!" Paul yelled.

Both Bree and Cody moved closer beside Paul, she said, "Dad, you are *not* a problem, remember that we are all here to help, and I will make sure everything is okay. Please settle down. If you don't, you know what will happen: its either hospital or the unthinkable. You've already had one cardiac arrest. Please stop!" Inside she was angry because Paul had gone on and on, but she could not show him that. She tried to reassure him things were okay, and she was on top of it all.

With that, she heard more utes arriving. Now most of the other blokes had girlfriends — nothing serious, except for Nick and Olivia — some said they would bring them tonight, but you never knew with them. Rick was a mechanic who owned an auto repair shop in Chilly, Nick was a carpenter and did jobs anywhere it took him, but Chilly was home. Josh and BJ were farm hands, otherwise known as jackaroos or stockmen; the description varies depending on the location and the size of the farm or station. BJ preferred the tag of jackaroo.

"Bree, do you need any food for tonight?" Beth asked. "I dug out five pizzas," answered Bree, "but I will put them on later."

Paul called out, "Both of you remember everyone's keys are to be put inside before you all start drinking, and remember you both have work tomorrow."

Bree's dad's mate had lost a son to drink-driving the

previous year. Since then, when the boys were over and they were partying—or if they had more than two cans of beer—Paul had made a rule: all keys inside.

Outside in the back yard, five utes were backed up in a circle towards the fire pit, Some had beds on the top of the tray of their ute, while others pulled out their swags and put them on the ground just under the back of the tray of the ute. Even though Bree thought this unsafe, the blokes would joke around saying, "Hey, 'Mum', its fine, anyway the keys to the utes will be safely inside."

Bree went into the house, "Dad, where is the tin for the keys?" she asked. Paul replied, "On the shelf near the fridge, and when you get all of the keys in the tin, please give it to me."

Outside again, Bree greeted the boys and had the tin can in her hand for the keys. "Okay you lot, hand them over, you know Dad's rule."

Josh remarked, "Where are your keys, Bree?"

"Already in here, Cody's too," she said, and she shook the tin side to side, the keys already in it rattling. And with that four sets of ute keys were dropped in the tin.

Cody offered to take them inside to Dad, as he always did. He would sneak a beer for Paul now and then, but it was always lite beer. This time he hid the can of lite beer in his coat before heading inside.

Josh was busy lighting the fire that Bree had set up for

them. Not too big a fire, enough though for them to cook on and to get some heat going. Bree could feel the chill in the air and knew that the cold front was moving in. She asked, "Do you guys want tarps to put up to keep the cold out? The weather report said there was a cold front coming through, and I can feel the chill in the air already." The guys who did not have the tent beds, said "Thanks, but we will be okay."

Josh brought out his metal wire cooker to cook some hotdogs, instead of sausages or steak, tonight. Rick brought out some of the delicious potatoes he had made. He would scoop out the centre of the potatoes, put ham and cheese in the middle, and then return the 'lid' to the top of the potato. He then wrapped each one up in tin foil so they could be thrown in the fire to cook through.

A short while later Beth came out with the pizzas, and Josh went to her and said, "Why didn't you yell out, Mum? I would have brought them outside for you." When she had put the pizza's down, Josh and the rest of the blokes came over and gave Beth a hug and said hello to her.

Bree was enjoying the get-together, but she had to remember not to drink too much. The talk was about the utes and what each one was doing to theirs to make it better. Rick was a mechanic, so they were always talking about how to make their utes run better or just sound better.

Rick said to Bree, "Oh, how are the new tyres going?" She replied that the tyres were good, just a bit of road noise, that was all. BJ spoke up and asked Rick about some suspension for rock climbing, and with that the blokes spoke at length about the suspension needed and the time it would take to put it on. Bree enjoyed four-wheel driving, but she was not into rock climbing or extreme four-wheel driving. Nick asked her, "When are you getting the bed for the top of your ute, and the awning for the passenger's side?"

Bree answered that if she had the money at 'tax time', she would do it then. 'Tax time' meant a tax refund. She realised she hadn't submitted her tax return and thought she had better put a reminder on her calendar for that, when the time came. She knew she would need a few thousand dollars, so she had to wait.

The next subject was the five-day trip away over the long weekend, coming up next month. Josh said his mate told him about a campground on a farmer's property about two hours away. It had showers and toilets for the girls, and it had a creek and some four-wheel drive tracks. Also they could have a fire, but it had to be contained. Josh said he would like to head out there for the five days: limited phone, no internet, just drive, relax, drink, and sleep.

Other places they all had been to before were thrown around. The one place everyone loved was a campground about three hours away. Very quiet, camping out in the open air, a shower and toilet block, and even a shop if needed—but it was expensive. There was a creek to swim in if it was hot, otherwise they could use the shower and toilet block.

It depended on the fire ban in the area at the time, whether you could have a fire or not. Now if you could have a fire, a drum was provided. But up in other areas, where larger groups would camp, there was a fire pit made of rocks and the area around the pit was cleared of grass. With only dirt around, the chance of a fire getting away was reduced in a big way. The only thing was, people had to collect or bring their own firewood, and sharpen their axes—no chainsaws allowed.

In the end it was decided to go to the campground where they had been before. They all really loved that campsite. Nice and quiet. Someone would have to take some firewood on their ute, just in case there was none when they arrived. Even though there were no four-wheel drive tracks at that campground, it was decided that a relaxing time for them all would be great—and well-deserved!

It was a challenge if they wanted to go four-wheel driving when they went camping, because the utes with the beds on their trays were parked up until they left to come home. So, if they wanted to go four-wheel driving they used camping tents instead. It was decided that later in the year, when it was warmer, they would do another trip to do some four-wheel driving.

Bree really wanted to go on the five-day trip away, but

she knew she could not leave the farm for that long. However, Cody had already spoken to Paul and Beth about her having some time off. They were happy about her going away, she deserved a break as she had been working hard for months with no time off.

"When do you all plan to go away?" Paul asked. Cody told Paul the dates, and thanked him for giving Bree time off. "Don't worry, I will get a mate's son over to check on the farm while she's away."

Paul and Beth came out and said goodnight to everyone. Dad thanked the blokes in advance for offering to help Bree the following day. They all said it was no problem, and if there was anything else they could do, all Dad and Mum had to do was yell out. Then Paul whispered in Cody's ear, "Thanks for the beer, Cody, it was great!"

CHAPTER TWO

Bree awoke early the next morning; she had not slept well. She did not go to bed until late—or rather, early morning. Throwing back the bedcovers she shivered, *'Oh my God, it's cold!'*, she thought. With that, she got out of bed and looked out her bedroom window to see a small plume of blue smoke heading skyward, empty cans on the grass, firewood here and there. The grass had a white look to it, so she knew there had been a frost last night. *'Gee, hope the boys were warm enough,'* she thought.

And then Bree said to herself. "Oh, what a mess out there! Oh well, coffee, shower, and clean up the yard."

Out in the kitchen Mum and Dad were sitting close to the stove with the oven door open, "Thank goodness for the combustion stove," Dad said. "Well, looks like someone had too much to drink last night, you got in late, my girl."

"Yes, okay Dad, I know, but I will be fine to do the work today," said Bree.

She knew her dad was right, but she had to get moving, she had to go and check the cows that were ready to calve. *'Oh, I hope there are no newborn calves, as they will feel the cold,'* she thought.

Bree and her dad bought the fifty-five pregnant cows to add to their herd of over five hundred head of cattle. New stock, new blood. She knew buying the cows was going to make more work for her early on.

With that, there was a knock on the back door and all five of her mates walked in.

'Oh no, I'm in my p.j.'s and Ugg boots!', Bree thought. *'Oh well, the blokes have sisters.'*

The blokes all got coffee and looked a bit worse for wear, hmm … too much to drink last night?

"I'm heading for the shower, then I'll need help cleaning the backyard up. Any helpers?" asked Bree.

"Yep, we will help," all the blokes said at once.

* * *

Bree came out of her room in jeans and a jumper, with a long oilskin coat in her hand. She said goodbye to her Mum and Dad, and headed out the back door. As soon as she came out of the back door, she felt how cold it was.

'Oh gee, that cold front really is cold!', she thought. Now she was really worried about the cows. Rick, Nick, BJ, and Josh cleaned up the yard and put out the fire. With

that, Cody and Bree headed to the shed, while the rest of the blokes headed out to get full loads of firewood.

Bree opened one of the big doors of the shed; it was large enough to have had many a party held in it—when it was clean! She thought to herself, *'I will have to clean the shed up for Mum and Dad's surprise wedding anniversary party, come late October.'* Although Paul and Beth's wedding anniversary wasn't a significant one this year, Bree still wanted to make a special effort. She was only too well aware of Paul's declining health, and she worried that they might not have many more anniversaries to celebrate.

The shed was many things: a party space, a wedding venue, somewhere to store grain, and a place for saddles and bridles as well as other horse accessories. The old shed had stood for many generations, but owing to its age, and most of the wood being rotten, it had blown down in a storm a few years ago. Paul had built the bigger, better shed the farm now needed on the same site. It was constructed out of high-tensile steel sheeting and had a concrete floor.

On one side, close to the front of the shed, was where the motorbikes and helmets were kept, and there was a cupboard full of medication for horses and cows towards the back of the shed on the other side. There was also a small storeroom that doubled as a spare bedroom when needed. Importantly there was a special pen where the pregnant cows could calve in safety.

Additionally, there was an open-ended shed next to the main shed, but this was used for storing hay and machinery. This structure was large enough for a tractor to be serviced or repaired in it. There was a cupboard full of tools on one side, and the petrol and diesel were stored closer to the main shed. Bree made a mental note that both the shed *and* the hay/machinery shed needed cleaning out.

Bree had been so busy with things, that now jobs on the farm were falling behind. She thought, *'I'm going to need help to clean it up, I'll have to ask the blokes if they will help me.'* But for now, she had to call Hayson, her black stallion, so she could get to work. She went out and let out a whistle for Hayson, so she could saddle him up to go and check on the cows. And maybe even enjoy a horse ride.

Hayson came galloping towards her; he knew he would get a carrot or two. Bree got her saddle and saddle blanket down off the peg inside the shed and put them on the stallion. He would blow up his stomach as soon as he felt the saddle sit on his back, so she would do up the saddle, walk him around then tighten the saddle up again. Hayson was a bugger for doing that, and she had come off many a time when she had not remembered what he did.

The black stallion could not be ridden by anyone else; Hayson was just her horse. Many of the blokes had tried to ride him and landed in the dirt. She thought she would have to change that now she was on her own on the farm. Dad could not ride anymore, but if the blokes needed a horse they should be able to ride Hayson. Oh well, mark it down along with a long list of other jobs.

Cody was just finishing saddling up Banjo, who was Paul's horse, but as he had a good nature anyone could ride him. After a good gallop across the flat ground, and checking fences as they rode along, they came to the paddock that the cows were in.

'Great,' thought Bree, *'no calves, hmm … let's see, there should be fifty-five cows.'* But she only counted forty-five. "Okay, let's go." They started by riding down towards the water trough in the paddock. No luck.

"Oh well, let's look up in the trees to see if they are up there," suggested Bree. Off they went, searching for the cows. While they were riding Bree was checking out the paddock to see how much grass was left for the cows to eat, and what condition the fences were in.

Cody pulled up, "Hey, what's up?" Bree yelled. But Cody gave her a thumbs up. After searching in and beyond the tree line, she found the ten cows. Okay great, found them! She pushed them slowly towards the main group. Cody helped her muster all the cows and started to push them towards the shed.

Because so many of them were close to calving, it was a slow ride home. Cody and Bree spoke about this and that, and joked about things as they rode, but she was always watching the cows to see how they were. She did not want to make them run; she preferred them to calve back in the special pen inside the shed, otherwise they were in the paddock behind the shed.

After a few hours of riding, it was a welcome sight to see the shed come into view. Cody rode ahead and opened the gate so she could push the cows into the paddock.

Now for the horses. *'Where are those three mares?'* she wondered. After a few whistles she found the three mares. At the back of the shed was another small paddock and she thought, for now, she would put the horses there. At least they had a bit of cover from the cold winds, as they could shelter behind the shed.

Cody said he would look after the horses. Bree thanked him while she brushed Hayson down. She put on the stallion's horse blanket because of the cold, and because he was so special to her.

Then Bree heard the utes coming back which meant the boys were back with the firewood. Now to the next job. The utes were backing up into the yard and Beth came out of the house saying to the boys, "Could I have some inside please?" A chorus of voices replied, "No worries, Mum, we'll bring some in."

"Mum, it's lunch time, do you still have the sausages in the fridge?" asked Bree. "I thought I might put the barbecue on and cook up the sausages to have with bread. Do you want me to do the onions, too?"

"Yes, that's a good idea. I still have the sausages, but I'll do the onions," Beth said.

After a few sausage sandwiches, Nick, BJ, Josh, and Rick headed home. Bree could not find Cody outside, so she went inside to find him. Paul and Cody were in a deep conversation, and her dad looked happy. *'Gee, Cody loves Dad. Hmm … what are they talking about?'* she wondered.

* * *

Sunday night was always roast night, complete with roast veggies, Dad's favourite. Tonight, it was roast pork, oh and the crackling, it was Bree's favourite thing! She could not wait for roast pork, roast veggies, and gravy, Mum always cooked it a special way.

Bree was setting the table when there was a knock on the back door and Cody walked through. "Well, what did we do to deserve the honour of you being here all done up like that?" she asked. Cody had gone to some trouble to look handsome for Bree.

Cody was showered and clean shaven, wearing a clean, ironed shirt open at the neck, which revealed his tanned chest. His clean jeans showed off his firm bottom cheeks and his long legs. It was really the first time Bree had noticed his body, and how tall, trim, and muscular it was. And it was the first time she noticed how sexy he looked, the muscles in his arms were well defined. The look of his whole body stirred something in her, and she couldn't stop looking at him. Bree took a breath in quickly, trying to keep her mind on the job at hand, but it was hard with Cody looking so sexy.

In comparison, Bree, was average height and slim, with blonde hair falling down past her breasts. Her face was fresh and youthful, her cheekbones were well-defined, and her sapphire-blue eyes sparkled.

Cody could only laugh, then he said, "Isn't it roast night tonight?" Paul came into the room and gave Cody a slap on the back, "Hi, son, how you are going? Hmm … you scrub up alright."

Bree did not know it, but Cody had strong feelings for her, however, he had not shown them or said anything to her. They were just mates, friends, even though he wanted more—but he was patient. They had known each other for a long time, and each of them had past relationships. But both those relationships had since ended and, unfortunately, not on good terms for either of them.

Cody could remember the first time he *really* noticed Bree, not as a fellow farmer or friend, but more like a man notices a woman. That day was last year at the annual rodeo, and at that time she was barrel racing on Hayson. He could not breathe when he first met her again. He remembered how beautiful she looked just in jeans and a shirt. Oh, and with her belt with the prize-winning barrel racing buckle that circled around her narrow hips.

Cody's last relationship ended over a year ago, and it

had been hurtful. Cody loved Bree's mum and dad, and he cared about their farm, The Flats. Even though Cody's family owned a farm not far away, his dad and three brothers ran it; Aurora Station was double the size of The Flats.

Paul and Cody were talking, and Paul asked if Cody could help around the farm. "Your family farm comes first, of course, but Bree needs help," said Paul. Cody said he would be there day and night to help her; he knew she was struggling with the farm, but he would help out, and Paul was to stop worrying.

The evening meal ended with, "Thanks, Mum — great meal!" from both Cody and Bree. They helped to clear the table and offered to wash up, but her mum said, "Thank you, but no, I am fine now. Off with you two young ones!"

Cody asked Bree if she would like to go for a night drive. "Okay, I'll just get my coat," she said. During the drive they spoke about their first meeting and laughed at some of the things that had happened over that year. Cody asked about her barrel racing and if she had thought about going back to it. Bree went quiet, and Cody realised what he had said. *'Damn, I forgot about that,'* he thought.

Barrel racing had been an issue back then, and Cody thought she was over it all. He knew how bad the breakup of her relationship had been, and the reason for it, which was why he was cautious of showing his feelings towards her. Cody parked the ute in a quiet spot, and he reached for Bree's hand.

"I'm sorry, I forgot about that. I'm always here if you need to talk." He wiped away a tear that had fallen down her smooth, firm face.

Bree moved over towards him and said, "Could you just cuddle me, please?" Cody held her tight by wrapping his strong arms around her body. He could smell her perfume and he could feel how slim she was. He wanted to kiss her so much, but he did not want to push his luck.

Bree felt secure in Cody's embrace, so she rested her head on his muscular chest. It had been a long while since she'd had strong arms wrapped around her and felt the warmth of someone's body. It felt so comforting, and she felt so protected—even though it was Cody, her best mate, who was cuddling her in her time of need.

He was so caring, and that made her feel at ease, but she was still upset by what had happened last year. She thought she was over all the hurt and the humiliation. Cody continued to wipe the tears that fell down her face and he held her tight while she sobbed. It hurt him to see her hurting like this, so he made a mental note to always be there for her and protect her. It was breaking his heart to see Bree so sad, but all he could do now was support her and offer to cuddle her when she needed it.

After a little while Bree stopped sobbing and sat up and said, "Thank you for the cuddle, I needed that."

While they were gone, Paul filled Beth in on his conversation with Cody. Cody had told him how much he felt for Bree, and he let Paul know he was protective of her. Paul had said to Cody, "I have already worked that out. Whatever you do, don't break her heart!"

Beth was happy to hear about the conversation, and she too had sensed Cody's feelings for Bree. All she could do was hope the relationship developed into something stronger.

CHAPTER THREE

Monday morning was always busy at the produce store, but Bree found this Monday busier than usual: horse rugs, feed, grain, and more.

The night before, when Bree and Cody were talking about the five-day trip away, Cody had said something, and she could not understand why he was saying it to her. He said, "You know I feel the odd one out with our group, all the other blokes have girlfriends, even though they're not serious, but *we* don't have partners." Cody added, "When we're all together I feel out of place, like I shouldn't be around. I dare say sometimes you feel like that too."

Bree thought it was an odd thing for Cody to say, when BJ did not have a girlfriend. He had 'girl friends', but nothing serious; BJ was a happy-go-lucky bloke. Happy in life, and happy either alone or with someone. She thought about how she, too, was the odd one out. *'Oh well, must keep working, I can think about that later.'*

After a busy day at work Bree came home and checked

the cows first to see if there were any calves born during the day, before heading to the house.

With a bang the back door was thrown open, and Bree raced into the kitchen, saying, "Mum, I have three calves on the way! I have my phone with me, so just leave my tea in the oven." With that, she took off in the ute up to the shed.

After an hour or so, and two calves later, Bree was having a problem with the third one. So she rang the vet, Scott, for help and he told her he was on his way.

When Scott got there he could see it was a two-person job to pull the calf out, so they worked together until the calf was born. A big-headed bull calf. The cow was fine, but she was exhausted.

Afterwards Bree asked Scott if he would like a coffee, and with that they headed for the house. Beth greeted Scott and poured two coffees. He said, "If you have any more trouble give me a ring," and with that he left.

The next morning Bree was up bright and early to check on the newborn calves. *'Gee, it is still cold!'* she thought. There was a frost on the grass that crackled under her feet. When she got to the shed, she saw that all the cows and calves were fine in their special paddock behind it. The calves were all feeding and doing okay, even in the cold snap. She thought, *'Damn weather! You cannot call it — one moment cold, next hot — and boy we could do with some rain.'*

Bree came across an old saddle in the shed when she

was looking around at what to do. *'Hmm … wonder who owns this?'*

After putting hay and grain out for the cows and for the horses, she headed to the house for breakfast, and took the saddle she had found with her.

Paul was at the kitchen table when she got back to the house, "Well, how are the three calves?" he asked.

"Fine, Dad, all feeding. I was looking around and had just started to clean up when I came across this old saddle. Any idea who owns it?" asked Bree. "It looks really old."

Paul took a big drink of his coffee and said, "It was your grandmother's, I had forgotten about it." Bree said she was going to take it in to town to the saddler to have it restored, as it was a beautiful saddle. Paul was not happy about it, but said nothing.

Bree was just like her grandmother—also a farmer—who had unfortunately died in a horse accident when Bree was a baby. Paul was still dealing with the death of his mother, because they had an argument just before she was killed. His mum had been on an unbroken horse she was not supposed to be on. Paul had never forgiven himself for not stopping her, and that was why he was so protective of Bree when she was working on the farm.

Bree got up from the table and said to her dad she was going out on Hayson to check the fences; she would take her mobile phone with her.

Saddling up Hayson, Bree could not stop thinking about her grandmother's saddle. *'Oh well, back to work, do not forget the rifle in case of dingoes and wild pigs — just get on with the job.'*

So Bree headed out on Hayson; riding the stallion gave her the chance to check the paddocks and fences and to see how much feed was left in the paddocks for the cattle to eat. Were there any fences that needed mending? Bree checked the water troughs to see if they were working properly. She was happy with everything so far, but made a note that the feed or grass was running low, and with the cold weather any grass would dry off because of the frosts and the cold winds. Just another thing for her to worry about. As a farmer, Bree had to make sure all the cattle had feed, and that they were alright. And paddocks needed their fences to be secure to keep the cattle in.

She was also looking for tyre tracks, the farm was a no-go area for kangaroo shooters or pig shooters. Paul did not like them because previously shooters had come on to the farm and wrecked fences, and they had shot cattle as well. So, the farm was definitely *not* open to any shooters.

However, yes, they occasionally shot the odd kangaroo or pig for feed for the dogs. Being a house dog, Risso was spoilt, Paul often would give him some steak, but otherwise he got dog biscuits and occasionally he would get special food from the produce store. Being the age that he was, and the amount of work

Risso had done over the years, Paul said he deserved good food in his later years.

Bree was looking at the paddocks and she could see how little grass there was for the cattle. Riding towards a tree line, Hayson started acting up. He was dancing around and rearing up, something was wrong. She held on as best she could, and when he settled down a bit, she dismounted; this was very strange for Hayson, as he was a quiet, well-broken stallion when ridden by Bree. Something was definitely wrong, Hayson never misbehaved with her.

Bree was concerned, so she started checking Hayson's legs and hooves. Then suddenly she heard a loud growl and looked toward the tree line. Oh no, dingo! Bree was taken by surprise, but she did not make any sudden movements, she quietly spoke to Hayson and tightened her grip on his reins.

Bree thought, *'You mongrel, you are not going to get the chance to kill one of my cows!'* Dingoes severely preyed on livestock in the country, killing—or worse—maiming them. This caused huge stock losses for many farmers, and shooting dingoes was seen as a humane way of protecting their animals—if it was done by experienced, skilled, and responsible operators.

Slowly, she reached towards the side of her saddle and retrieved her rifle. Carefully and quietly she loaded the rifle; dingoes have excellent hearing so it had to be done silently. Tightening her grip on Hayson's reins, and whispering to him, she aimed the rifle towards the tree line and fired. She still held the reins tightly as Hayson moved away from her quickly, but she was lucky he settled down enough for her to mount him.

Still with the rifle in hand, Bree quickly checked the area where the dingo had been. It had gone for now, thank goodness, but it would be back. But Hayson was still acting up, so she kept talking to him as they started towards the direction of home. As they got further away from the tree line he started to settle down, but he was still galloping fast. Bree finally settled the stallion down to a walk, and she kept talking reassuringly to him.

When Hayson sensed home, he started into a gallop again. Bree let him have his head this time, she knew she had not had a chance to ride him much lately — because of work at the produce store, and all the other things that needed to be done on the farm — so he needed the exercise. Bree was enjoying the ride, she loved the fast gallop and feeling the wind in her hair. The freedom of riding on Hayson was the only thing that cleared her mind and helped her to feel better emotionally, mentally and physically.

Bree made a mental note to get some help so she could check out where the dingo was now. She knew from all her years on the land: where there was one — there would be more. She would have to talk to Cody about the situation and ask if he would help her. Bree knew the next time she headed out towards that area it

would be on the motorbike. Even though she preferred to ride Hayson, the motorbike was a better op-
tion in this instance.

When Bree saw home she rode straight to the house.
Hayson deserved a feed of nice, green, sweet grass.
She let herself in through the side gate of the back yard
and rode Hayson around the house to the front yard
and tethered him there temporarily. First things first
though, Bree stepped inside briefly and locked her
rifle away safely in the gun cabinet, and then went
back to Hayson. Having heard some noises, Paul came
out on to the front steps to investigate, and when he
saw that it was Bree he said to her, "Boy, Hayson is
putting on some weight there girly, looks like he needs
more exercise … or you go back to barrel racing." Bree
replied, "Firstly, Hayson deserves some nice, green
grass, and to the second one: no! I have finished barrel
racing, never again will I do that … and you know
why, Dad!"

* * *

Later, sitting on the verandah and having coffee, Bree
told her dad about the fences and the grass, and what
they should do. Then she told him about running into
the dingo, and how Hayson really played up. "I will
give Cody a call to come out with me tonight in the ute
to have a look," she said.

Paul was not happy that Bree had been on her own and
he said, "No more going out there on your own,

Brenda!" Brenda was Bree's full name, and he only used it when he was angry with her. No matter what she said, he had put his foot down: no one was going out there alone.

'Here we go again,' Bree thought, *'He doesn't trust me! Why not? I can ride, I can shoot, I take care of the farm — what else does he want me to do?'* With that, she angrily marched towards the door on the verandah. When she reached it she opened the door and held it, she turned towards him with tears falling down her face and asked, "When will you see that I am a grown woman, able to take care of myself? You raised me to take care of myself and the farm. Why can't you just trust me?!"

With that, Bree ran down the steps, jumped up on Hayson, and gave him a good kick in his side. He went straight into a gallop and jumped the fence. Bree did not know where she was going, she was just riding, and she was hurting from what her dad had said. Anytime she was distressed she found it helpful to gallop on Hayson. Ride fast, ride long. Nothing to concentrate on but riding; it always cleared her mind.

Hearing the loud, angry voices Beth came out to the verandah and asked Paul what was going on. He told her about the dingo and how he worried about Bree. Paul explained to Beth the argument he had with Bree and how upset she had been. Beth said, "When are you going to stop? Bree is capable of dealing with dingoes and everything else on the farm. *You* taught her how to deal with everything." Beth added, "If you don't stop, there won't be a farm, because everyone has a breaking point. You make me so angry at times, I'm going to ring the doctor and talk to him about you. Paul it is enough! Where is Bree anyway?" Paul replied sheepishly that Bree had jumped on Hayson and galloped off.

Paul knew he had gone too far, but he worried about Bree, he knew the dangers of being on the land and what could happen. He knew she had given up a lot to work the farm, but she was still his little girl, and he knew he had hurt her this time. With that, he rang Cody and spoke to him about everything that had just happened.

Within a few minutes Cody came through the back door. "Hi, Mum, are you okay?" he asked Beth.

"No, Cody love, I am not. Paul has gone too far this time and Bree is really hurting. I have not seen her jump on Hayson and take off jumping fences like that for over a year. He needs to stop his stupid controlling and let her run the farm. Sorry, son, I'm upset and worried about her, you know what she's like when she gets hurt."

Cody gave her a cuddle and said, "Don't worry, Mum, I'm here now, and if you want anything you just yell out. Have a cry, you'll be okay."

Beth cried, and after a little while she pulled away from him and said, "Thank you, son. How about a coffee? ... and only two sugars!"

"Okay, Mum, yes two sugars. Where's Paul?"

"He's on the verandah, in his chair. I'll bring out your coffee in a minute."

Cody went out onto the verandah and sat next to Paul. "Hi, Paul," said Cody, staring at him, "Well you have really stirred everything up this time, haven't you?"

Paul put his head in his hands, he could not look at Cody. "What have I done, son?" asked Paul.

"Paul, yes, it's unfortunate you have your heart condition, and you can no longer do what you love, working your farm," agreed Cody. "Your two sons might not want anything to do with it, but Bree does—she loves the farm. You taught her everything she knows, and she's more than capable of managing here. Gee, she's working the farm, and working in town as well. Your view on what she can do, and cannot do, is now affecting everyone."

Cody continued on, "You must let go of the reins. If you don't stop this, she will walk, and then where will you be? You'll lose the farm! You must decide here and now: back off and let Bree have the authority to run the farm, or sell up. Paul, I apologise for talking to you like this; I said nothing before, out of respect for you, but now it's affecting Mum too. Beth is hurt that you won't accept that you have a heart condition and that your controlling behaviour disrespects Bree, and all that upsets Beth even more. Because of what you said to Bree and the *way* you said it she has taken off riding, and Beth and I are worried about her."

Beth had come out onto the verandah with Cody's coffee and heard what he said to Paul. She said, "Cody's right, it's your choice what happens, but you better make your decision before Bree gets back here. Enough is enough!"

Paul said angrily to both of them, "Do you know how damn hard it is for me to sit around and not do the things that need to be done? Do you know how I feel? Yes, I know I can't do some things, but it's hard to give *everything* away!"

Beth stood up with her hands on her hips, "It's either Bree runs the farm, or you in a box! Now, what's the decision?!"

Paul was quiet for a while, then he said, "Bree can run the farm, I will still be here for her, but she has the final say on what to do. She is going to need help because those lazy sons of ours sure won't help!"

Cody spoke, "I spoke to my Dad about this before I came over here, and he said that I was to help Bree on the farm. He also said that he was proud of her, with everything she had done already, and if he can help, he's only a phone call away. So, I will be here day and night to help Bree run the farm."

Cody turned to Paul and asked directly, "Paul, is it Bree's farm or not?"

"Yes, it *is* her farm," Paul replied.

CHAPTER FOUR

Bree had been riding for over an hour when she turned for home; the sun was now in the western sky, so sunset would be in a couple of hours. She still had tears pouring down her face from what her dad had said to her earlier.

Bree wondered what she was going to do. Her brothers wouldn't help out, and units for rent in town—well, there were none. She really did not know what she was going to do, but she had to do something because she couldn't keep going on like this.

Bree arrived back at the shed, finally. She unsaddled Hayson and gave him a wash down, as he had been sweating, then she brushed him and led him into his paddock. She sat on an old chair that was in the shed and was trying to think what to do, but she got no answers. Bree was still upset at Paul. *'Oh well, I better head to the house,'* she thought. As much as she did not want to get into round two with her dad, she had to go to the house, she needed a drink and something to eat as she had missed lunch.

Walking down from the shed Bree noticed Cody's ute, *'Why is he here? He was supposed to be helping his dad today,'* she thought. She walked through the back door and was taking off her boots when Beth called out, "Is that you, love?"

"Yes, Mum, it's me," answered Bree. She walked into the kitchen and Cody came towards her. He cuddled her and wanted to know if she was alright, but she backed away and said she was fine—just tired. Bree needed something to eat, but in that moment a cuddle from Cody was the last thing she wanted, so she headed to her bedroom.

Beth followed Bree to her room, "Are you all right, love? I know your dad went too far today. We had a big talk to him. When you are ready could you please come out, as we want to talk to you." Beth put up her hand to stop Bree from talking, "No love, you need to hear this; I know you're hurt and upset, but you need to hear what your father has to say. Remember, I was here for you when everything happened last year, and I know how hurt you were then. Are you okay?"

Beth sat down on Bree's bed, and she answered, "Mum, I can't take any more of Dad controlling me with the farm, and really, this has brought back all the feelings from last year. I thought I had dealt with all that stuff."

Beth cuddled her daughter and said to her in a quiet voice, "You know your mum is always here, and I know you're still hurting, in a big way, from what happened last year. Cody and I have spoken to your dad and laid down the law with him. When you are ready come out, but wash your face first, okay?"

With that, Bree cuddled her mum and thanked her for her understanding. She would wash her face and be out there shortly.

"Mum, can I have a coffee please?" she asked.

"Sure," Beth answered.

Beth returned to the kitchen and spelled it out plainly, "Now you listen, Paul, and you listen up good, Bree is still hurting. If you do anything or say anything to upset her, well—your bed is still in the shed. And the same for you Cody. Bree is really hurting."

Now, in their many years of marriage there had been only one other time Paul had slept in the shed. Too much drinking had scored him a night of sleeping there, and he wasn't keen to do it again.

Bree washed her face and gave her hair a brush, then went out to the kitchen where Beth gave her the coffee. They were sitting at the kitchen table when Paul spoke up, "Sweetheart, I am sorry for everything I have said, and how I make you feel … make out you're not able to run the farm. Mum has said her piece to me, and so has Cody. It was what I needed, as I should never have made you feel like I have done."

Paul continued at length, "Your two brothers have

abandoned me by not wanting anything to do with the farm. Now, I am letting you have full control over it, but your Mum and I will still be here for advice, or anything else you need."

Before Bree was able to respond, Paul went on to acknowledge that she had done a great job so far with the farm, but there were only so many hours in a day to do all the jobs needed, so Cody had agreed to be Bree's 'farmhand'. Paul explained that he, Cody, and Cody's dad, Thomas, were all in agreement on this new arrangement. And that Thomas had said to say how proud he was of Bree to have run the farm so far, and that if he could help in any way, he was only a phone call away. At the end of his explanation, Paul asked Bree, "What do you think of all of this?"

Bree was glad she was sitting down, otherwise she would have fallen down. She could not believe someone had finally gotten through to Paul.

Bree answered in a calm voice, "Thanks, Dad, for the apology, and yes, I *was* hurt—big time. Thank you for seeing that I can run the farm, but I know I need help as the jobs are piling up." She continued on, "Cody as my farmhand—well I couldn't ask for a better one. But, Dad, if you overstep the mark, and I tell you to back off, will you? I don't want to keep going through this every time."

Beth spoke up, "Sweetheart, Cody and I have spoken at length to your dad, and if he oversteps the mark or says anything, well, then either Cody or I will say something too. Your dad still has his bed in the shed — if he interferes, that's where he will be sleeping!"

Paul put his head down, then looked at Bree, "I am sorry, so sorry. I haven't seen you and Hayson jump fences like you just did in a long time. Tomorrow I'm going to start the paperwork to put the farm into your name — if you agree. I will still be here to help if you need it, but the farm will be yours. Okay?"

Bree couldn't believe what she was hearing — *her* farm! Oh, what would her brothers say? It was everything she wanted — to have the farm in her name.

Bree said to Paul, "Dad, I'm so thankful you're giving me the farm, but there are two problems: I don't have the finances to run it — *and* what about William and Jeff, won't they want part of the farm?"

Paul replied, "Where money is concerned, your mum and I will be your financial backers, but the only thing I ask is we talk beforehand about selling cows, the market prices, things like that, okay? If you agree, then I will arrange for a solicitor to get the papers drawn up."

Paul added, looking at Bree, "Your brothers walked away years ago and have never been back, you have given up your dream so you could be a farmer. So, if your brothers have anything to say, they can deal with the solicitor. Okay?"

With that, Bree got up and cuddled her dad and said,

"Thank you!" She then cuddled her mum and whispered in her ear, "Thanks, Mum, I love you."

They all had dinner together, and after clearing the dishes off the table Bree said she wanted to go and check the cows because of that dingo. Cody told her to hang on, he would grab his rifle from his ute and come up with her. Bree went to the gun cupboard and got out her gun and put a night scope on it, then she unlocked the ammunition cupboard and took some bullets out, and lastly she locked up both cupboards.

This was not the first year that dingoes had been a problem; she could remember when she was a small girl a dingo came close to the house. They decided to drive up to the shed in her ute, just in case they needed it for any reason. When they got near, they turned towards the paddock with the cows and calves in it. The handheld spotlight she kept in her ute, plus the fixed spotlights on her ute gave them plenty of light. And the lights around the shed were like spotlights as well, so nothing could hide around there.

After checking the shed, they jumped back into Bree's ute and went for a drive. After about an hour of driving around, without spotting any dingoes, they headed back to the shed.

On checking the pregnant cows, Bree saw that another two were ready to give birth, so she herded up the two cows and put them in the pen in the shed. Cody sat with her during the calving, keeping a close eye on the two cows. Both calves needed some help being born, and they worked together to pull them out and safely deliver the two big calves.

Suddenly Bree stopped, she touched her ear, as much as to say 'listen'. Cody heard the noise as well. Luckily, both of them had brought their rifles out of the ute, near to where they had helped the cows give birth. With rifles loaded, they both went quietly to the back door of the shed which was ajar, and Bree spotted the dingo trying to get to the rest of the pregnant cows. With a dead-eye left-handed shot, she killed the dingo.

Hmm … this one wasn't the one Bree had seen earlier. She was worried now for the pregnant cows after finding a dingo so close by. She wondered how they missed seeing the dingo when they were out there earlier. *'Well, they are smart animals,'* she thought.

Suddenly there was a car pulling up at the shed, it was Paul and Beth. "What the hell has happened out here?!" demanded Paul. Cody explained what had happened so Paul settled down. Satisfied that everything was fine, Paul and Beth returned to the house.

Then Cody phoned Josh, Rick, BJ, and Nick and asked them to come out to The Flats to help them look for any other dingoes. Nick couldn't make it as he had an appointment, but the others all turned up, rifles in their utes. After some discussion it was decided that they would all head out to where Bree had met up with the dingo when she was out riding Hayson.

While heading out, they would all do a sweep to see if there were any more dingoes close by. If they saw anything they would get on their UHF radios and tell the others.

After a few hours they arrived back at the shed and everything was quiet: the horses with their rugs on, and the cows and calves were settled in their paddock. With that, they closed the doors and headed back to the house.

"Well, did you lot see any more dingoes?" asked Paul.

"No, Dad, we didn't," replied Bree, "and we went right out to the old stockyards and back."

The old stockyards were between the house and the back boundary. It took about three hours to drive from the shed to the back boundary if the creek was down. Ten Mile Creek ran through the farm, through adjacent farms, and then it ran through town.

The old stockyards were over halfway from the shed to the boundary. It took a couple of hours on a motorbike to reach either the eastern or western boundaries. The house sat at the front of the property, and the shed sat close to the house. A big enough farm for Bree to run—but too much for one person.

Back at the house, Bree said goodnight to everyone and went to bed, as she was tired. Tired from crying, and tired from the big ride on Hayson. You could say she was exhausted emotionally and mentally too, just like last year when she split up with her ex-boyfriend.

CHAPTER FIVE

"Morning, Mum, coffee please!" Bree said as she entered the kitchen the next morning. "I'm heading to the shed to check on the cows and calves, and then I'm jumping on the motorbike to check out the eastern boundary fence alongside Penny's property."

"Make sure you have your phone, and you have your rifle or pistol with you," replied Beth. "The Pennys lost three cows to dingoes last night. So please be careful."

Then she added, "You can't wait for Cody to come and give you a hand?" That question was answered by a stare from Bree.

"Okay, but he better hurry up or I will head out without him," said Bree. Just then the back door burst open, and Cody came through in a hurry, "You're late for work!" she said to him.

Cody apologised, "I'm sorry I'm late, had to talk to Dad about something."

Bree ordered, "Okay, grab your gun, we're heading out on the motorbikes this morning, we've got to check over the paddocks first."

Beth spoke up, "Cody love, the Penny's next door lost three cows to dingoes last night, so if you see one … well, you know what to do. Oh, have you both got your phones on you?" The two of them assured Beth they had their phones on them, and they left to go and check the cows and calves before heading out towards the boundary fences.

After an hour or more checking the boundary fences Bree and Cody returned and went straight to the house to tell Paul that they hadn't seen any dead cows or any dingoes.

They then headed to the shed. Bree got to work deciding which paddocks to put the cows and calves in, as the cold front had now passed. It was still winter, and the weather was cool, but not as cold as it had been.

Bree decided she could move the cows and calves out further away from the shed, but still close enough for her to check on them. And she would let the horses out in a paddock. *'Let's hope they will be okay while I am at work at the produce store,'* she thought.

* * *

The five-day trip was coming up on the weekend. After working the week at the store *and* on the farm, and the goings-on with her father, Bree was looking forward to the five days away. Paul told her it was fine; she should go on the trip as she deserved a break from the farm. She was cleaning out her ute when Cody arrived all loaded up for the trip. He drove his faithful Landcruiser ute, it was an old model that had a bench seat up front.

He suggested, "Why don't you put your stuff in my ute? Save running yours."

Bree thought about it, and asked jokingly, "Well, where am I going to sleep?"

Cody answered, "We can share the bed, if you are okay with that. I'll stay on my side." Hmm … she wasn't sure, but she decided it would be okay *if* he stayed on his side of the bed.

Then all the others turned up, some with their girl-friends. Of course, BJ was on his own, but he didn't mind that if he was having fun. Rick had some fire-wood on his ute, and BJ had some as well. Bree hoped there was more firewood at the campground, but she had packed her sharpened axe in case they needed it. Paul had sharpened it earlier in the week for her.

They all said goodbye to Beth and Paul and, of course, Beth came out with more food for all of them. Bree and Cody told them where they were going for the five days, and approximately when they would be home. Bree gave her mum her ute keys and said if there were any problems to please call Thomas.

With that, they all left on a well-deserved five days away. Driving with Cody, Bree felt so happy, she would often take a quick look at him and think of her own feelings for him. They joked around about this and that, and after a while she drifted off to sleep. Cody watched the road, but he took a few quick glances at Bree as she slept.

When they got to the campground, they all had to sign in and give the manager the registration numbers of their utes. They were then given the rules and were told they could set up in the usual spot they did when they came to these campgrounds. While they were at the office the girls all visited the toilets. From where they camped to the toilets was a good walk, but not so far that you needed to drive down to them. Sometimes they did though, as driving seemed easier.

They all drove up to where they were camping and decided to put the utes in a circle, or sort of circle. The firewood was unpacked from the utes and thankfully there was plenty provided so they didn't have to go looking for any extra. BJ got the fire going, while the cooking gear and Eskies were unpacked off the utes. Someone turned on some music, not loud, but just enough to be heard. Josh started to get lunch under way. He threw on some sausages and Rick's girlfriend, Charlotte—who everyone called Charlie—buttered the bread.

It was so relaxing sitting in the shade of an old gum tree, the sun was shining through the leaf canopy and a gentle wind was blowing. The weather was lovely: not too hot, not too cold; Bree was feeling sleepy, but she didn't want to go to sleep, so she got up and made a coffee and checked the fire. The blokes were all sitting around the fire talking about their utes again. They seemed to talk about nothing else.

Bree and the other girlfriends felt left out, but it was the first time she felt *really* left out. And it reminded her of what Cody had said about feeling left out too. The other girlfriends were talking about their relation-ships—and what was wrong with their relationships. She felt truly left out of *that* conversation.

Later, Rick got the dinner going and the all the girls walked down to the amenities block for a shower. The dinner was yummy, and everyone thanked Rick for the tender home-grown steaks and the delicious, fresh salad he had brought along. After a while Bree said her goodnights to everyone and headed to bed. As she started up the ladder to go to the tent bed on Cody's ute, she said to him, "You better stay on your side of the bed!" This was met with laughter and joking. Everyone there knew that Cody and Bree were not a couple, but they couldn't pass up the moment to tease both of them.

Cody was a gentleman and kept to his word, even though he definitely wanted to cuddle Bree's slim, firm body. It was difficult, but he knew not to rush things, especially as he sensed she was still hurting from what her dad had said, even though she wouldn't come out and say it. Plus he didn't want to blow his chance with her.

But damn, Bree was so gorgeous and *so* sexy, he found

it hard not to cuddle her. He thought sadly, *'Gee, I have three more nights of this!'*

A couple of days later the group all sorted out about getting into the utes that didn't have tents on top to go four-wheel driving on a neighbouring property. Rick had arranged it with the owner, who was fine with it, but they had to shut any gates they opened and were not to chase the cattle.

They all enjoyed four-wheel driving through the mud and getting dirty. Back at the campground the girls all headed for the showers, and the blokes elected to try out the creek. The blokes went in, but came out quickly as the water was freezing! The days were beautiful, not hot, and not cold, but the nights had a chill to them. Bree was thankful for the thick, big doona on Cody's bed on the back of his ute.

On the second last day all the girls decided to go for a walk to check out the rest of the campground and see what wildlife was around. They were walking along chatting and laughing when a ball landed at Bree's feet. She picked it up and her gaze fell on the person who had kicked the ball. Shocked, Bree gasped and dropped the ball. It belonged to a little girl, who she guessed was about three years old, and Bree's ex-boyfriend, Bob, was standing next to the girl! The little girl was the spitting image of Bob. He stared back at Bree and neither one said a word.

Olivia knew everything that had happened last year

between Bree and Bob, so she moved beside Bree, grabbed her hand, and turned her around away from him. Bree was as white as snow, and she was now having difficulty breathing. Olivia was worried that Bree was going to pass out. She couldn't talk or even respond to Olivia. The girls were trying to guide Bree to a picnic table away from Bob and his daughter.

Olivia was really concerned for Bree; she didn't look well at all, so she rang Nick and told him what had happened. Nick and Cody drove down there in Nick's ute straight away. It didn't have a tent on top of it, so it was perfect for Cody to pick Bree up in his arms and lift her into the tray of the ute beside Olivia and the others. Then he jumped up into the tray of the ute and held Bree. Bob witnessed all of this, but said nothing to his wife, who was there with him too.

Back at camp, Cody sat Bree in a chair and got some water for her. Olivia had not left her side. When the others asked what happened, Olivia told them, and they all asked Cody what they could do. Cody asked, "BJ, can I borrow your swag for a while?" BJ replied, "No worries, where do you want it?"

"Could you please set it up between your ute and my ute, I want to give Bree some privacy."

With that, BJ and Charlie set up the swag, and rigged up a curtain between the utes. When they had finished, Charlie went over to Cody and said, "It's all set up, Cody. Is Bree okay, can I do anything else to help?"

Cody thanked her and he said, "Can you open the curtain up for me, please? Also, can you get me some water and a washer. I'm going to stay with Bree".

Cody never left Bree's side, he sat with her, wiping her face with a cool, wet washer, and then he placed it gently on her forehead. Then he lay down with her, protecting her as he had always done. Her breathing had become regular again, and her colour was returning, but she was still very quiet. And when Cody asked her if she was okay, she didn't say a word. Finally, she drifted off to sleep. After a while Nick put his head around the curtain and motioned for Cody to come outside.

"Hey, Cody," whispered Nick, "Rick, Josh, BJ and I went down and paid that low life a visit, we even helped him pack his car and leave. His wife knew nothing about Bree, so I told her everything and, well, I would hate to be in that car heading to wherever they live. Let's just say that bloke won't show his face around here or Chilly ever again!" Nick paused to let Cody take it all in, and then continued, "Olivia rang Beth — out of concern — and Beth said just to let Bree sleep, that there is no need to cut your trip short, and to give her love to Bree."

* * *

It was dark when Bree woke up, and she was trying to get her bearings when Cody put his head around the curtain. He lay down beside her, "Hey, Bree, how are you feeling now?"

Bree asked, "How did I get here … what time is it?"

Cody asked if she remembered what had happened, and she said she remembered seeing Bob and a small child … and after that—nothing. Cody explained everything, including Olivia phoning Nick, and how they went and picked her up, and that they made up BJ's swag for her and put up the curtain for privacy. Cody told Bree that the group was really concerned about her, but she didn't have to worry because Bob was escorted out of the camp by Nick and a few others.

Bree cried, and Cody held her tight.

"Hey, it's okay, I'm here, and nothing is going to happen to you," he assured her.

He was amazed then that Bree reached out and hugged him tightly. After a minute or so Cody helped Bree up and out to a chair. Olivia came over to her and hugged her, and Bree said, "Thank you, Olivia, for everything."

Olivia apologised for telling the group about what Bob had done to Bree a year ago, and what happened today, but she knew it was the right thing to do. Bree thanked Olivia again for helping her, and said it was probably best that everyone knew, and that she no longer had to hide the truth.

* * *

During the previous year Bree had been in a serious

relationship with Bob. He lived in Braham, but worked around the whole area as a farm supplies sales representative. Bree and Bob met at the produce store when he was on one of his regular weekly trade visits. Working away from home allowed him to keep his marriage hidden from Bree. It started well between them, but as the months progressed he became increasingly violent towards her, and she knew she would have to end it with him.

Bree competed in the barrel racing at the rodeo that year, and easily won her event. Bob and Bree had an argument because she was attracting attention after winning the barrel racing. He took out his frustration on Bree with his fists, and beat her badly in front of everyone there. There would be no going back to him after that.

She was seriously injured, and broken physically, mentally, and emotionally. To make matters worse, she had not known she had been in the early stages of pregnancy, and suffered a miscarriage the day after the beating. Bob mysteriously suffered a beating of his own later that day and was run out of town, never to be seen again, until that day at the campground.

While some of the facts were common knowledge in town, only Beth, Paul, Olivia, and Cody knew the *whole* story. It was the reason why the four of them were so protective of Bree.

* * *

Bree was waking up more and enjoying the coffee Rick gave her; he promised there was nothing 'additional' in the coffee, in a joking way.

Bree told Olivia that she wanted to go to the toilet, and asked if she would drive her down to the toilet block and stay with her. "Not a problem, I will get the keys from Nick."

The girls arrived back to find dinner was ready. Bree found she was hungry — well, she had slept most of the day because of what had happened.

Tomorrow they would head home: wake in the morning, pack up the utes, and make sure the camp area was left clean.

* * *

It was dark when Bree and Cody arrived home. The ute was dusty and muddy, as they all did some four-wheel driving on the way home. When they pulled up at the house Beth and Paul came out to greet them. Beth remarked, "No mud or muddy boots inside, please!" Bree kicked off her boots outside the back door and tiptoed through to her bathroom so she could get cleaned up.

Meanwhile, Cody brought in all her bags. It gave him a chance to talk to Beth about what happened, and how Bree handled everything. Beth thanked Cody, and asked him if he wanted to clean up here or go home. "No, I'll head home, unload the ute and clean up, and then I'll come back over later. I'm still worried about Bree. Thanks, Mum." Cody added, "I will grab a coffee, though, when I come back."

Cody went home to Aurora Station, and a few minutes later Bree emerged from her bathroom, cleaned up after the dusty trip back home. Beth and Paul asked her about the trip and were told *all* that went on — *especially* about Bob. Paul threatened, "He never wants to turn up here!" Bree didn't know it, but Cody was furious at the campground because of Bob, and he was thankful for the other blokes handling the situation. It showed how much Bree meant to them all.

CHAPTER SIX

Monday already, the start of a new week, boy that last week went fast, and it was *another* busy morning at the produce store. Olivia popped in to see how Bree was, and reminded her that if she ever needed to talk—or just needed someone to listen—all she had to do was to call her.

Bree replied, "Hang on, Olivia, I want you to have this. I'm so thankful for all that you did for me at the campground." As a thank you, Bree gave Olivia a one-hundred dollar note. Olivia said she couldn't take it, but Bree said, "Put it towards getting your hair or your nails done—my treat." Olivia thanked Bree, gave her a hug, and said, "That's really kind of you, but you know you don't have to do that."

Work on the farm and at the produce store was constant, and it kept Bree's mind off Bob and what happened at the campground.

Later that morning when it wasn't so busy, Bree noticed a poster up on the board outside the produce store. Chilly's Annual Rodeo and Ball was in three weeks' time. The town came alive when the rodeo was on. She would have to look at the stock to see if there was going to be enough of what they normally sold out of when the rodeo was in town. Hmm … better order some grain, hay, some halters, and more rope.

* * *

After work Bree told Beth and Paul about the poster, and her mum asked, "Well, are you going to the ball this year?"

Bree didn't go last year because of the beating she had received from her then boyfriend, Bob, and she was in no shape to be around happy couples. She thought she would go this year, but she needed a partner.

"I am thinking about going, but who will be my partner?" Bree said to her mum, as she headed towards her bedroom. With that, her dad yelled out, "Oh my goodness, girly, sometimes you need to take off the blinkers, and see who really feels for you and would do anything for you!"

The next minute her dad was on the phone, "Hi, Cody son, are you going to the rodeo ball this year?"

Cody replied, "Yes, I was going to ask Bree if she would go with me."

Paul called out Bree, "Will you go with Cody to the ball?"

Bree yelled back, "Yes!" but shook her head trying to not say anything to her dad for ringing and asking

Cody to the rodeo ball on her behalf.

Now that a date for the ball had been sorted, the next problem was a dress. *'Hmm … me in a dress,'* Bree thought. Just then, Beth knocked on her bedroom door and asked Bree about the dress. "Mum, I don't know, I don't really have a dress good enough for the ball," she replied.

"Dad and I will take you shopping next week, okay?"

Bree turned to her mum and said, "No thanks, Mum, it's okay, I can pick something up in town this week, or maybe I'll go over to Braham where there are better dress shops. Plus there are shoe stores there, and I could look at makeup as well."

Bree had thought long and hard about Bob, and she had decided that if he could move on with his life, well, so could she!

Work was extra busy with all the additional people in town who were organising the rodeo, as well as all the regular farmers. Plus, people from further out came to town to take part in the rodeo or to watch it, and attend the ball too. All the available accommodation in town was booked out.

Bree headed to Braham to look for a dress and shoes for the ball and—for the first time in a long time— some makeup. She looked in many dress shops, until she found a beautiful, three-quarter length midnight blue dress that made her blue eyes really stand out. The neckline emphasised her cleavage, and the shoestring straps crossed over low on her back revealing how slim she was.

Then, she tried on a pair of shoes that she thought would suit the dress. They had straps across the toes and around the ankle, and the stiletto heels were high and slim. Bree thought, '*Hmm … how am I going to walk in these?*' When Bree had put the shoes on, she went for a walk in them. After a few shaky attempts, she finally got the hang of walking in such high heels, and enjoyed how they made her even taller.

"Okay," Bree said, "I will take them both."

While still wearing the new dress and shoes, she looked in the mirror and thought, '*No one will recognise me at the ball!*'

* * *

Beth and Paul had great fun at the rodeo and stayed for a while, as Paul enjoyed talking to all the farmers. However, Bree did not go the rodeo with them, as it was still too soon after the events of the previous year.

So instead Bree stayed home to get ready for the ball. She wondered if she looked alright in her new dress, and if she had put on her makeup correctly. She even let all her long wavy hair cascade down over her breasts for once. She had been lucky to find a dress that fitted her like a glove: it showed off her slim figure and it really showed off her cleavage and her small, firm breasts. *Hmm … I think this might stir a certain bloke up tonight. I wonder if it's too much?* she thought. She was in half a mind to just put on jeans and a shirt, where she thought her trim body and her firm breasts were always well hidden.

She walked out to the lounge room to show Beth and Paul, but she hadn't heard that Cody had arrived. Mum cried, "You look so beautiful, my darling!" Dad was wiping his eyes. Bree said, "Dad, what's wrong, are you okay? What's wrong with the dress?" Paul said he had never seen his little girl look so beautiful.

Cody was quiet, he couldn't take his eyes off Bree. His heart skipped a beat when he saw her walk into the lounge room. He had never seen her look so gorgeous and so sexy. He found it hard to breathe, but he managed to tell her how beautiful she looked, and that he was honoured to be her partner at the ball.

They said goodbye to Beth and Paul as they headed out the door. Cody had cleaned his ute out, washed the interior, and put on car seat covers. He helped Bree up into it, and caught a glimpse of her long, slim legs. Again, Cody was dumbstruck.

When they arrived at the hall it looked like everyone had turned up for the rodeo ball. Rick and Nick were there with their girlfriends, Josh was there with a date, and BJ … well BJ was on his own usual, but he was happy just to be there. When Cody helped Bree out of his ute, all their mouths fell open in surprise to see her in a dress, with her hair down, *and* makeup on. A few even let out wolf whistles, Rick stared in amazement,

Josh had just taken a big mouthful of his beer that he spat out in surprise, and BJ was standing back with his mouth open.

They were used to Bree in jeans and a shirt and boots. Nick came forward and said, "I'm Nick, and your name is …? And what are you doing with *this* bloke?" She laughed and gave him a punch on the arm. No one in the group could believe how gorgeous Bree looked.

Other people at the ball were amazed when they saw Bree too, they had never seen her look so beautiful! Because she was always in jeans, a shirt, and boots at work, they never saw how stunning her figure was or how attractive her face was.

Cody was always protective of Bree, but more so now, and even when his mates came close to her, he gave them a stare as much to say, 'back off!' A few blokes came up to Bree and asked for a dance, but she kindly refused. Bree and Cody had a few dances together that night, she enjoyed dancing with him because he was surprisingly a good dancer.

As the night wore on the older people left, leaving the younger generation to keep partying. Bree had caught up with old school friends, and also chatted to Rick's and Nick's girlfriends, and Josh's date. Olivia asked how she was going after the five-day trip away, and she was pleased to hear Bree was doing fine. She couldn't resist asking, "*Please* tell me where you got that beautiful dress from!"

Olivia then, jokingly, said to the others, "When was the last time we saw Bree in high heels? Hmm … never? Well, just check out the heels tonight!"

Olivia turned to Bree and said, "Boy, girl you have gone out fully. And, damn, you look sooo good!"

Cody came over and asked Bree for a dance and, naturally, she accepted. It was a slow dance, and Cody held her tight to him. He whispered in her ear how beautiful she looked and how he had to be her bodyguard because so many blokes were checking her out.

Cody's arms tightened around her slim, firm body, and being taller than Bree, he caught a glimpse of what was down the front of her dress. The neckline was low, so not only her cleavage was seen, but when he held her tight, he could see her firm, small breasts. He had to keep himself in check as hormones started racing through his body. Bree's arms tightened around Cody, and she loved the feeling of cuddling his strong, muscular body.

After what happened at the campground—she saw that Bob had definitely moved on—Bree decided enough was enough. She was moving on as well, and some people would be surprised by just how much. Being held tightly in Cody's strong arms felt so good, and she felt so much warmth towards him. She could smell his aftershave and noticed how nice it smelt. She could feel how fit and how muscular he was, and she let her hands run all the way down his back and then felt his tight and sexy bottom.

The dance ended, Cody held her hand, and they walked over to the bar for a drink, when Bree noticed the time. But she thought, *'To hell with it, I'm enjoying myself for a change.'*

Next, they were on the dance floor again to another slow dance, and this time Cody gave her a peck on the cheek. She turned her head and kissed him back, then Cody held her close, and they kissed some more.

Nick touched Olivia's arm and said, "Well, check that out will you? Maybe Cody isn't the fifth wheel in our group anymore. I'm so happy for the both of them." Word spread in the small group about Cody and Bree on the dance floor.

Cody had to keep himself in check as his hormones where really awakening now, hmm … not yet, too fast.

Just before 1 a.m. Bree and Cody headed for home. When they arrived home, he helped her out of the ute, but they didn't walk inside, they headed around the back of the house to the logs near the fire pit. Cody put a blanket on the logs for them to sit on, and another one around Bree's shoulders.

Cody said, "I enjoyed the night, and I hope you did too. You look so sexy in that dress, and I don't think you realise what it does to me." Bree grinned, and Cody cuddled her for a while, and they sat and looked at the night sky. The stars were so bright. No noise, just peace. Both of them were enjoying this moment.

A little after 1.30 a.m. Bree said she had better go to bed, so Cody saw her to the back door. He said good night, and gave her a kiss on the cheek and a cuddle, and said he would call her in the morning. Not long after she got into bed, she received a text message from Cody thanking her for the night and reminding her how beautiful she was.

Bree was floating with the clouds, she found it hard to fall asleep. Her thoughts were about Cody and how he made her feel. She finally drifted off to sleep thinking of the dances they had shared that night.

* * *

The next morning Bree walked out to the kitchen, "Hi Dad, hi Mum." Paul and Beth looked at one another then looked back at Bree, "Morning, how was last night, many people at the ball?" Paul asked.

"Yes, there was a good turn out, and I enjoyed myself," answered Bree.

They all heard a knock on the back door and Cody walked through, "Morning, Mum and Dad, good morning Bree."

Cody and Bree left to go up to the shed, and hopped in Bree's ute. When they got there Bree looked around at what to do first. They had to start to clean up the shed so she could accurately see how much hay and grain they had. She looked around and thought, '*What a mess! Oh well, got to clean out all the old hay, it's a fire hazard.*'

After a while—and a lot of work—Cody said he needed to go home to do some chores, but he would be back tonight. Bree asked if he would like to come early, and they could drive out and watch the sunset. Cody answered, "Yes, that would be beautiful."

So, Bree got busy getting her ute ready for them to go and watch the sunset. Her ute had fold-down sides on the tray, racks front and back of the tray, and a toolbox that went across the tray behind the cabin. She found the old foam mattress in the shed that she used to sleep on in the horse trailer when she competed in barrel racing. Bree cleaned the tray out and rolled up the mattress and put an old doona on top of it as well as a blanket, in case it got cold later.

Bree was looking forward to tonight, she had a shower and put on clean jeans, but the shirt she decided to wear had a lower neckline than usual. She got together some drinks and something to eat, and put them in an Esky and loaded it in the back of the ute.

Cody turned up all showered, shaved, and smelling beautiful; Bree wondered what the after shave he wore was, as she loved it.

They headed out towards the old stockyards. There was a small hill, with trees that stretched along the top and down each side. A quiet, private spot for them to park and watch the sunset. The trees were leafy, and so they offered shelter in winter and shade in summer for the cattle.

Bree parked her ute up with the tray facing the sunset. Cody was surprised to see the mattress and pillows in the back, but helped her set up the bed in the tray anyway. He thought the time had come for him to get the courage up to talk to Bree about taking their relationship further.

The sunset was beautiful, the sky was coloured orange and pink, and there were a few little white clouds as well. When the sun set, the sky turned black with stars all shining. Bree said she loved the western sunsets, they always had beautiful colours.

Cody turned to her, "I'm just wondering about something, and I want to ask you a question," he said.

She turned to him and said, "Okay, I'm listening."

"You know we have known each other through some difficult times, and we've had some great fun, but after the rodeo ball I want to know what you are feeling towards me," he said, while stroking her hair.

"Yes, we have been there for one another in the past, and you really helped me when there was no one else," Bree started. "I loved the rodeo ball and I will admit I do have feelings for you. I know it's time for me to move on with my life, but I'm frightened—as you well know—because of what happened last year."

Cody said, "Well, we both feel the same about one another, and at last I can tell you how I feel about you. Bree, I have strong feelings for you, I know you are cautious, and I really don't want to hurt you." Cody continued on, carefully choosing his words, "I don't want to do anything you don't want me to, I just care about you so much."

Bree leant on one arm and put her other arm around Cody, "I have strong feelings too, and I don't want to do anything to hurt you either, but I don't want to go through again what I went through last year. I know *you* would never do that to me — it's just me."

Bree leant in to Cody and gave him a cuddle. He was hoping for more, but he decided to let her make the moves. After the cuddle they both lay stretched out looking up to the sky.

Cody grabbed a drink for Bree, and one for himself. He asked, "I'm just wondering, and you tell me please honestly, hmm … how do I say this? …"

"Oh, my goodness, just spit it out! You know we can talk openly about anything."

Cody leant closer and put his arm around Bree and rubbed her back, "I'm nervous, okay. I'm wondering if you are ready to … "

She moved in closer to him and said, "Please be patient with me. Yes, I've guessed — felt — your hormones were running a-mile-a-minute. All I ask is patience, please. It will happen, but just not now."

Cody responded by wrapping his arms protectively around her slim body. Finally, they pulled apart, and Cody whispered, "You just say the word or give me a sign when you are ready."

She gave a little laugh and smiled at him while holding his clean-shaven face, "The question you couldn't come out and ask me was, if I was comfortable for you to make love to me."

"Yes, that's true. But only when you are ready to, Bree," said Cody.

She sat up and leant back against the toolbox, "You helped me through the pain last year, and you know what happened. I haven't been with anyone since. As much as I want to say yes, I don't know if I can handle it just yet. I'm sorry."

Cody turned to her and looked into her eyes while holding her hand and lightly brushing the hair from her face, "I know what happened, and I wish I could take that pain away from you. You don't need to be frightened anymore. What about we put that on the back burner for now and you call the shots? You do what *you* are comfortable with. How does that sound to you?"

A tear ran down Bree's face, and Cody wiped it away, "I never want to upset or hurt you."

She reached out and held his face in her hands, "I couldn't ask for a more loving and patient person, thank you, Cody."

There was nothing more that needed to be said by either of them. And so they lay down together on the mattress in the back of the ute, held each other close, and looked up at the millions of stars shining brightly in the night sky.

CHAPTER SEVEN

The following day Bree started work in the shed again, there was still a lot to do to get it clean. *'Where do I start?'* she thought. *'Well, I'd better start somewhere!'*

Bree was busy sorting out the saddles and halters when Cody arrived.

"Morning, how are you going, Beautiful?" he said, and he greeted her with a cuddle and a peck on the cheek. She said she was good, better now he was there, and she hugged him back. Cody asked Bree what she wanted him to do.

"Can you start to clean over the other side of the shed please?" she replied.

With that, he went to work. After a few hours of them both working steadily, Beth came up with coffee and biscuits for them.

"Gee, you have done a lot of work, you two," said Beth approvingly. "Morning teatime, though."

Beth looked around and saw how much there still was to clean up and she offered to come and help them when Paul went for a rest.

"Thanks Mum, if you want. You don't have to though, we can manage it," said Bree.

Beth looked at the floor, and Cody asked, "Mum are you okay? What's wrong?"

Beth sat down on an old chair, her shoulders were slumped and she looked sad. She said "I know Paul can't do any heavy manual work anymore, but lately he is really getting to me. With his moods and the way he talks, sometimes I could kick him out of the house to live up here!"

Bree agreed with her mum, and said she thought it was time that her dad saw the specialist again, he was getting worse.

Cody and Bree both gave Beth a hug before she returned to the house.

"Mum doesn't go to CWA meetings much anymore because of everything she has to do with Dad," said Bree. Cody understood Bree's concerns, and said he thought it was time for the specialist too, even if Beth only phoned him.

Bree had sorted the saddles and halters, and noticed they needed a wash and were in need of some oil in the leather. She was moving a saddle when she found — underneath all the other tack — her old barrel-racing saddle. She dropped it and just stood there staring down at it.

Cody noticed her standing there and came over to her and asked if she was okay.

"I, … I just found my barrel racing saddle, and … and it brought back memories of what Bob did to me," she stammered.

Cody led her over to a hay bale and sat her down.

"Hey, look at me. What he did was over a year ago now, and you have a lot of friends who are supportive and protective of you." Cody kept talking, "Instead of the bad memories, why don't you think of the good memories you have with that saddle? Like when you won your buckle."

Bree reached out and gave Cody a cuddle and whispered, "Thank you." Without another word being said, they went back to work.

Bree arrived at the produce store the next morning and said good morning to Phil, the owner. She then spotted on the notice board that there were rodeos in the surrounding areas in the months to come. She knew she would have to check their supplies again.

It was now mid-August, and every night—for about a fortnight—Cody and Bree would drive out to their spot and watch the sunset, or if it was later in the day, they would just pull up and spend time looking up at the clear night sky. Just spending time together talking, laughing, and enjoying each other's company.

Bree was becoming more comfortable with Cody, and

she would often just lie with him in the back of the ute and cuddle him. One night they were enjoying the clear night sky, and there was a gentle wind blowing, it was not a cold winter wind or a summer wind, just a cool evening breeze. Out of nowhere they heard gun shots. Bree went to sit up, but for her safety Cody pulled her back down to lie flat on the tray.

"Where are those gun shots coming from?" she whispered to him.

Cody pointed in the direction of the eastern boundary. It was then that Bree could see headlights and spotlights. She couldn't make out if it was a ute or a car, but Bree wanted to go toward the lights. Cody whispered, "No, just watch them."

In silence they lay on their bellies and watched over the top of the tray side to where the lights were. After about an hour the lights headed off toward the eastern boundary. Once they were sure that they had gone, Bree and Cody sat up.

"Let's head over to the eastern boundary" Bree suggested as they jumped into the front of the ute. Cody was unsure, but he said okay, and asked if Bree had her rifle in the ute.

"Yep, let's go!" she said, and with that she swung the ute around and turned the high-beams on, and all the spotlights as well.

When they reached a paddock at the eastern boundary, Bree noticed the boundary fence had been pushed over. Bree was furious!! She pulled the ute to a stop quickly and grabbed her rifle and ran to the two cows lying on the ground. Both had been shot numerous times and one was still alive. She had to do the difficult thing of putting the animal out of its suffering.

While Bree was looking after the cows, Cody had grabbed the torch from the ute and walked in the direction the lights had gone.

He spotted two kangaroos; both had been killed and left on the ground. From the tyre tracks it looked like the vehicle was a ute. He walked back to Bree's ute and saw Bree putting her rifle back in the rack. She was angry and said she would be ringing the police when they got back to the house.

Cody grabbed the UHF radio and called up Rick, Nick, and Josh. Rick answered and Cody told him what had happened. Rick said he would get the word out to everyone he could. Cody told Rick that he and Bree were heading back to the house to ring the police, and asked that if Rick found out anything could he come out to the farm straight away.

When they got to the house Bree pulled up the ute with a squeal that caused dust to cloud up from underneath. Beth came out of the house and Bree walked straight past her with her hand in the air. Cody told Beth what had happened. He asked Beth if she had a gun handy at the house as he had the feeling these blokes where out-of-towners and he was worried for her safety. "Son, I have my gun and yes, we'll be okay." She laughed as she added, "Hey, I can swing a cast iron frypan pretty good too!"

Cody pulled his mobile phone from his pocket and went out to the verandah and phoned his dad, Thomas, and told him about what had happened. Cody added that he was going to stay over at Beth's and Paul's as he was worried for their safety. Thomas agreed that was the best thing to do, and asked if they had phoned the police. Cody replied that Bree was doing that, and he also told his dad that Bree had lost two cows so far. In the morning, he would be going out in his ute to check the herd, and he would have to mend the fences.

After taking all of this in, Thomas said, "I will be over at Beth's and Paul's in about half an hour." Then he added firmly, "Don't go back outside!"

Paul had been dozing inside, but woke up with all the noise, and came outside. "What the hell is going on, a man is trying to sleep!"

Cody told Paul all that had happened and what was being done now, and also that his dad, Thomas, was coming over.

Bree rang Sean, the local police officer, "Sean, I'm sorry to disturb you so late, but I want to report that some low lifes have busted through our boundary fence and come onto the property. They've shot two cows so far. One was dead, and I had to put the other out of its misery." She continued, "Cody was with me, and he found two dead kangaroos as well. These blokes were loud and driving crazy. Cody believes they were in a ute, but colour-wise we don't know."

"You're not the first farmer to ring in tonight. The Pennys just phoned as well, they've lost cows and have fences damaged too," confirmed Sean.

Harrison Road ran between the Penny's farm and Bree's farm, The Flats. It was a bitumen road that ran on to other farms as well.

"The shooters have come off Harrison Road. Call me tomorrow morning and let me know what other damage there is," Sean said. Then he added, "I don't want you and Cody's mates going out looking for them. Give me a day to ask around."

Frustrated and angry, Bree replied, "*Maybe.*"

Just as Bree finished the call, Thomas arrived. Paul and Beth greeted him in the kitchen.

"Would you like a coffee, Thomas?" asked Beth.

Thomas smiled, "Thanks Beth, I will take you up on that." He turned to Paul and Beth and said, "Boy, these kids certainly make you worry, don't they?!"

"That's part of the reason why I'm grey," Beth chuckled. "I'm glad Cody was with Bree, otherwise I know she would have chased those blokes."

Paul added, "Bree has just got off the phone to Sean, and he says the Pennys have lost cows as well."

Thomas offered his help in any way he could, he told Paul and Beth he wanted to make sure they were safe.

Beth said, "Let them come inside, they will have a headache and a half!" With that Beth swung the cast iron frypan around and they all laughed.

Thomas said, "I would feel better if Cody stayed the night with you, if it's alright. I know Bree is very capable, but I am just worried that's all."

"Thomas, thank you. Cody is welcome any time, and I would feel better with him here too," replied Beth.

The next morning, just as the sun's rays were colouring the sky, Bree and Cody set out in her ute to check out the damage. Bree could see more clearly now how the eastern boundary fence was flattened where those blokes had driven over it. She followed the track they had made in the grass and they came across another dead kangaroo and two more dead cows. She was furious!! "That's four new cows gone now, and they were in calf!"

Bree was so mad she smacked the bonnet of her beloved ute with her open hand. The force of it put a dent in the bonnet. Cody put his hands on her shoulders and said, "Enough! Hitting out like that is not going to fix the problem."

Bree answered back, "If I see them, I will make them pay for what they have done!!"

Cody knew Bree was outraged, and he had to try to

settle her down before she did something that was reckless. After a few minutes and a cool drink of water, Bree rang Sean.

"Add another kangaroo and two cows to the damage, plus fences. Have you heard anything at all yet?"

"You and the Pennys, and four other farmers got hit last night," responded Sean. "I'll ring you when I find out something, okay? I'm sorry for the damage and the cows. I *will* find out who did this."

Bree and Cody worked all of the rest of the morning fixing fences. Then Cody brought the tractor down so he could bury the cows that had been killed. Leaving them in the open would only invite dingoes, and wild pigs too.

In the afternoon Bree announced that she was going into town. "Do you need anything in town, Mum?"

"No thanks love, you be careful please. Is Cody going with you?" asked Beth.

"No, he's not coming with me, and I *will* be careful, thanks Mum."

Bree went straight to the pub to see Johnno.

"I heard about last night, are you all doing okay?" he asked Bree.

"We are okay, but I lost four good cows and some fences were damaged. Now, if anyone knows any-thing it would be *you*. It seemed like these guys had had too much to drink," said Bree.

"I know you; you *can't* go after these blokes Bree, leave it to Sean!" Johnno warned her.

"Like hell! I'm going to find these blokes and teach them they can't do this to me, or any other farmers!" Bree said angrily.

Jenny came into the bar and said, "Hi" to Bree and offered her a drink. She took Bree to a table to sit down to talk, and to try to calm her down. While Bree was talking to Jenny a bloke walked up to her.

"If you are looking for those idiots, they came from Huntsville, and they have caused plenty of damage up there too. One of their daddy's is a barrister in town and he's been getting away with everything," said the bloke. He introduced himself as Nigel, and Bree asked if she could have his phone number, as she — like other farmers — didn't have the money to keep fixing fences and buying cows.

With Nigel's phone number in her hand, Bree thanked Jenny and headed to the produce store.

"Hi Phil, what ammunition have you got for a .243 calibre rifle?"

"What are you up to, Bree?" he asked, out of concern.

"I'm low on ammunition and just want to make sure we have enough on hand … nothing special."

After completing her purchase at the produce store, Bree picked up a few things at the grocery shop and then headed home.

CHAPTER EIGHT

The next day Bree went to work at the produce store and all the talk was about the idiots and the damage they had done, and how many cows had been killed. Sean came into the store to see Bree and told her he had made enquiries about who was responsible, and that he had contacted Huntsville police station for more information.

"So that's all you have done?!" said Bree. "Have you spoken to Johnno at the pub, or anyone else? Why haven't you gone and arrested those idiots?"

Bree was fuming like a scorching-hot summer's day!

She finished her shift and was heading towards home when she noticed an unfamiliar ute parked outside the pub. It had spotlights right across the top of the cab and beer stickers all over the tray sides. The ute was dirty and there was a large amount of mud in the back tyre wheel arch. She had a feeling it belonged the idiots who had caused all the trouble.

When she arrived home she noticed that Cody's ute

was parked up at the shed.

"Okay, Sean is as useless as a wet paper bag! I'm sure I saw the idiots' ute at the pub when I was leaving work. Will you help me please, Cody?" she asked him.

"What are you thinking?! *You* can't do anything," Cody said, expressing his concern. "You will put yourself in danger. Don't you remember the number of guns they had? And it looked like they were really drunk too!"

"Hear me out first," reasoned Bree. "The paddock on Harrison Road is where they came in. So, if we all line up in our utes on the edge of the tree line, with the lights off, we wait for them to come in, and *then* we turn all our lights on. Each one of us is standing with the driver's door open and rifles pointed in their direction, but not *at* them." She took a quick breath and continued, "We get them out of their ute and use zippy ties — which are better than rope — to tie them to the bullbar. When we have done that we'll ring Sean to come and pick them up. Please, Cody, help me with this!" Bree pleaded.

"How will you get them to come onto the property?" asked Cody.

"All I have to do is ring Johnno at the pub and tell him to 'accidentally' let them know about an easy target of cows and kangaroos," she said.

'*Oh, damn!*' thought Cody, '*sounds good, but risky.*'

"Okay, I'll call the boys and we'll get set up, but what about your mum and dad?" Cody said.

"We'll tell them we're just going out checking the farm for intruders, that's all," Bree answered.

With that, Cody called up the boys. He explained the plan and said it was up to them if they took part, but all of them said yes, they would be there. They all agreed to meet up at Bree's shed.

Cody and Bree got to work on their utes to make sure all the lights were working, and Bree even hooked up an extra spotlight on her driver's door.

She rang Johnno to ask if the blokes were still there in the pub. Johnno said, "Yes, they're still here and they're getting noisy. A few aren't getting any more to drink either. Why?"

Bree asked Johnno to 'let slip' to those blokes about the easy targets of cows and kangaroos at The Flats. Johnno said what she was planning was crazy, and she really shouldn't be doing it, but he would let the blokes know.

Josh, Nick, Rick, and BJ arrived at the shed, and they had prepared their utes as well. It had just gone dark, so they all headed off to the tree line; they were more than ready for those blokes to come in!

While they waited, they had something to eat and drink, only using a small torch for light. After a while Bree saw lights in the distance, and now they were getting closer and closer.

"Here we go!" she said, and with that they all went to their utes and got ready.

Bree had her night-vision scope on her trusty .243 rifle. The powerful spotlight was all set up on the driver's side door of her ute. The six of them had their UHF radios on, waiting for the word from Bree.

They saw the lights approaching even nearer now, and then they heard the sound of an engine getting closer and closer. And then over the UHF came Bree's clear instruction: "Light them up!"

Blinded by the many lights targeted at it, the ute stopped dead, and one of the blokes in it yelled out, "What the *hell* is going on?!"

With her rifle trained on the ute, Bree ordered them, "Out of the ute, now! Put all your guns on the bonnet!"

The blokes just laughed and stayed in the ute. She could see that there were two blokes in the cab of the ute and three standing on the tray. Bree calmly took aim and shot the front passenger's-side tyre of the blokes' ute; with that one of them jumped out of the passenger side of the cab, and he was swearing loudly.

"I told you lot to get out of the ute and put your guns on the bonnet—and you didn't listen. There are six rifles loaded and pointed in the direction of your ute, so get the hell out NOW!!" Bree yelled.

Cody was worried because Bree was getting angry.

The bloke who jumped out of the ute called Bree a cow, so she let off another round, this time at the back tyre.

Now one of the three blokes on the tray of the ute held his rifle in the air, and then slowly got down from the back of it. He cautiously put his gun on the bonnet and then moved to stand at the back of the ute with his hands on his head. Then the remaining two on the tray followed his lead and did the same.

The bloke doing all the talking said, "Leave us alone, cow, we can do what we want!" Bree turned on the spotlight on the driver's door of her ute, which partially blinded the 'Mouth'.

"Look, you dog, if you don't do as I have asked —" and with that, the Mouth went for his gun, at the same time Bree let a round go and it also hit the front passenger-side tyre, as the previous shot had done.

The Mouth quickly raised his gun above his head and then carefully placed it on the bonnet and moved away to join the other three. Then the driver slowly got out of the ute and did the same.

"Right! The five of you are going to walk towards my lights, NOW, and lie face-down. Refuse? … well …"

The Mouth was laughing and was telling the others that the bitch was bluffing. Straight away the boys each let off a shot, so now the back tyres had many bullet holes in them, too.

Four of the blokes moved, but the Mouth didn't, so

now Bree was white with rage! "MOVE now!!" she screamed … and still the Mouth laughed. She shot out one of the spotlights on top of the blokes' ute and finally the Mouth moved.

Bree asked the boys to zippy-tie the blokes to the bullbar of their ute. They all started to walk in the direction of the five blokes. When Bree was close to them the Mouth stood up suddenly and moved towards her. Because she had been physically attacked by Bob, her ex-boyfriend, Bree reacted instinctively and went into defence mode. She still had her rifle in her hands; Cody was beside her, and then the Mouth called her a bitch again.

Bree handed Cody her rifle, and with a closed fist she let fly a punch straight to the Mouth's stomach. He bent over as the punch winded him, but then he stood up and he called Bree a cow again. This time she had really had enough, and the *next* punch sent him flying backwards. He was out for the count!

Josh, Rick, Nick, and BJ zippy-tied the other four backwards to the bullbar of the idiots' ute. Then Josh took the rifles off the bonnet, and the rifle out of the cab of the idiots' ute, and put them on the tray.

Cody asked Bree, "Are you okay? I have never seen you fight before. Remind me never to fight with you, otherwise I'll be like the Mouth here." Bree didn't answer, instead she turned the Mouth over on to his front and zippy-tied his hands behind his back and his ankles together.

Nick came over to Bree and said, "Holy hell! I didn't know you could fight! Remind me never to pick a fight with you." He asked her, "Are you okay? How is your hand feeling?"

She replied that she was okay, but admitted that her hand was *killing* her. Nick went to his ute and got out some ice from his Esky and wrapped it around Bree's hand. Bree thanked Nick, and said she had better ring Sean to let him know that she had caught the idiots.

Bree dialled Sean's number, and he answered on the first ring. "Evening, Sean. Could you bring the police van out to The Flats?" Bree asked the policeman. "Come to the Harrison Road side, you'll see all the light from our utes."

"What the hell have you done, Bree?!" demanded Sean, sounding angry.

"See you in twenty minutes or so," Bree said briskly, and ended the call.

The Mouth was now waking up. Now that they could all see more clearly, BJ recognised him, and saw that the Mouth was Douglas Brighton Jr. and he told the others who he was.

"Your days are numbered. I will come back and finish you and then I'll burn your house down!" Brighton Jr. spluttered out at Bree.

Bree went over to him and leant in close and said

firmly, "The only place you're going is jail, and Daddy won't get you off this time." Douglas spat at her, and in response she took her boot heel and slammed it into his 'crown jewels'. He winced in pain, and she leant down to him and said if she ever saw him in Chilly again he would live to regret it.

Douglas Jr. knew he had met his match and just lay curled up on the ground. One of Douglas Jr.'s mates called Bree over to him.

Noticing this, Douglas Jr. yelled out, "Shut up, Aaron!" but Aaron ignored him.

"Yeah, what do you want?" she asked.

He mumbled, "I apologise for all the damage done to your place. I would like to offer you money as restitution." Bree said she would talk to him tomorrow at the police station, and she remembered he was the first one to give up his rifle and stand on the ground with his hands on his head.

CHAPTER NINE

After a few minutes they saw the flashing lights of the police van approaching.

Bree knew Sean was going to be mad at her, but she didn't care. She had caught the blokes who had caused a lot of damage in the area.

"Brenda Douglas, what the hell have you done, and what have you five blokes done?!" demanded Sean. She looked at Sean and stared hard at him, and in a deep, angry voice replied, "No one other than my father calls me Brenda. Got it?!"

The Mouth said something crude, so Bree walked over to him and threatened him, "This heel won't go on your crown jewels this time, but on your face. Shut the hell up, or do I need to raise my foot?!"

Sean pulled her back. The Mouth was screaming, "Help me, Mr Police Officer, she's mad!" But Bree just lifted a knee up.

"Cody, can you put the Mouth here in the van, please?" Sean asked.

Bree turned to Sean, "Don't you mean Douglas Brighton Jr? He is the main offender in all of this."

Cody picked up Douglas Jr. and cut the zippy tie around his ankles, and immediately he tried to run for it. Now, both BJ and Josh played rugby league, so the tackle was a 'textbook' one that even brought a smile and a laugh from Sean.

Then BJ, Josh, and Cody took Douglas Jr. to the back of the police van, and Cody was left alone with him. Cody leant against Douglas Jr. and warned him, "If you ever come near Bree or the farm again, you won't be breathing! And I will deny I ever said that to you — got my drift?!" Then Cody gave Douglas Jr. a good push that made him land face-first on the floor of the police van.

Sean changed the zippy ties for handcuffs, cuffing their hands in front of them, and as he did, he read the apprehended blokes their rights. Then he led them altogether to the back of the van. He hauled Douglas Jr. out and told the others to get in. When Sean changed the zippy tie for handcuffs on Douglas Jr., the handcuffs were fastened behind his back. Sean read him his rights and put him back in the van.

Josh and Rick came over to Sean with all the blokes' rifles. Because they were bolt-action rifles, Josh and Rick had taken the bolts out to make them safe, and they noticed that all the magazines were *full* of ammunition. These blokes had come prepared to shoot and to keep on shooting!

Sean stored the rifles safely behind the front seat of the police van, then Josh handed him the keys to the blokes' ute. Sean asked if one of them would drive it back to town, and Josh said, "Sorry Sean, not possible, you'll need a tow truck, the front and back passenger tyres, as well as the spotlight on the top, have been shot out."

Sean put his head down and said, "What have you done, Bree?!"

Josh answered for her and said, "Let's just say I will never get into an argument with her when she is mad!"

Sean shook his head from side to side. Then he and Josh heard voices coming from the van. They peeked through the air slats of the van to hear one of the blokes telling Douglas Jr. he was an idiot for thinking they would get away with it. Douglas Jr. said, "If you had done as I said to we wouldn't be in this van!" Sean thought, *'Thank you, now I definitely know who is the ringleader of the group that has caused all the damage'*.

Sean told Bree, Cody, Nick, Rick, Josh, and BJ to go home. "And no more shooting, lock up your guns. I will contact each of you for a statement tomorrow."

He then turned directly to Bree. "Bree, you're going to get into trouble one day for the things you do. From now on stay out of police business!" Sean said sternly.

Cody moved closer to Bree and put his arm around her

and said to Sean, "Don't worry, she'll behave herself."

Bree and the boys headed to the house to tell Paul and Beth what had happened. Bree knew her dad was going to be mad, but she knew she had to do something. The loss of four cows, and potentially four calves, was going to hurt.

Paul was awake when they arrived back at the house. The expression on his face told her how angry he was. Beth welcomed them all into the kitchen and asked, "Coffees all around?"

Bree was locking her rifle in the gun cabinet when Paul started. *'Oh no, here we go again,'* she thought.

"Dad, shut up, please, and let me explain!!" Because of the intensity and anger in Bree's voice, Paul was shocked and sat down.

Bree told him of the lead up to the events of the night, and how no one was to blame but her, as it was her idea. She told him what happened, and also what happened when Sean arrived.

Paul was not happy, and he turned to Cody and said, "You let her do this. I really thought you would have stopped her." All the blokes started laughing, and Paul interrupted them asking "Well, what's so damn funny about that?"

Nick said, "Paul, in all the years I have known Bree, I have never ever seen her so angry. God help anyone who gets on her wrong side!"

Josh added, "It was entertaining watching that idiot take on Bree, though. I wonder how he is feeling after her boot heel went into his crown jewels?"

Beth said, "Bree, what did you do? I thought I raised you better than that."

Bree told Paul and Beth what the Mouth called her, and what she did in response. Paul had his head down, with a slight grin on his face, and all Beth could do was look at Bree in disbelief.

"Mum, can I have an icepack from the freezer please?" asked Bree.

"Why do you need an icepack?" asked Beth. Nick told Beth how Bree had given the guy a 'bunch-of-fives' a couple of times. Beth examined Bree's hand. All the blokes looked too, and were amazed at how red and swollen Bree's hand was.

"Can you move your fingers at all?" enquired Beth.

"Yes, Mum, a bit, I just need to put ice on it to get the swelling down."

Cody rang his dad, Thomas, and told him what had happened. Thomas couldn't believe what Bree had done, and he was happy she was okay.

The next morning Bree rang Sean to see when she could go in to give a statement.

Sean replied, "You can come in this morning, and I will take your statement. For now, I'm giving you a directive to take any firearms out of your ute and lock them up. No firearms are allowed in your ute, other than if you are on the farm and doing farm business." Bree agreed to this, and about two hours later she arrived at the police station with her right hand bandaged, thanks to Beth.

Sean took Bree into an interview room and enquired, "Are you alright? Have your broken your hand?"

Bree answered that, no she hadn't broken her hand, it was swollen though, and it was really painful.

"Sean, I want to apologise for last night. But I had to do something to protect my property and the rest of the farmers in this area." Bree continued, "As a farmer, losing four cows to drunken idiots who have no care is gut-wrenching. And from what I've found out, they have done this at Huntsville too, and the Mouth's daddy, Douglas Brighton Sr., keeps getting him off any charges."

"You do realise you can be in so much trouble for what you have done … and Cody and the blokes can land in trouble as well. I don't agree with what you have done at all, but I am going to put you on a warning." Sean added, less severely, "One thing though, where did you learn to shoot like that?"

"I learnt to shoot like that from Mum and Dad, and from being on the farm. And I agree with you, only on the farm will I ever carry my rifle or use it," Bree said.

"Do you have a gun cabinet at home?" Sean asked.

"Yes, we do. It's bolted to the floor, and we have a separate one for bolts and ammunition," Bree answered.

"Okay, Bree … your statement, can we start? Tell me everything from the beginning," ordered Sean.

Bree told Sean everything, and at the end of it she asked him if she could talk to one of the blokes, in Sean's presence. Sean agreed and asked, "Which one?"

"I only know his first name, Aaron," admitted Bree, "but I would recognise him if I saw him."

Sean showed her the mugshots, and Bree pointed out the bloke she wanted to speak to, and Sean went and got him from the holding cell.

"Sit down there," said Sean to the bloke when he returned with him to the office.

Bree said, "Hello. I promised I would talk to you at the police station, and here I am."

"Hi, my name is Aaron James," he said to Bree, and then he addressed Sean, "Mr Police Officer, could you take this down, please?"

Sean prepared to document the conversation.

Facing Bree, Aaron said, "I want to apologise to you for the damage, and for the pain I have caused you. I admit to shooting one of the cows, and I wish to give you money to replace it. I am so very sorry."

Bree considered this for a moment, and then she said, "Aaron, thank you for the apology, and for admitting to shooting one of my cows, but what about the other farmers who have been affected?"

Aaron replied, "I will personally apologise to all the farmers and, as I don't have a lot of money, I am willing—if the court allows me—to work on every farm to pay back the debt. I don't care what I have to do. I know I got mixed up with the wrong people, and that ended last night." He took a deep breath and continued on, "I want to change, and I am willing to do whatever I need to do to make that change. I lost my dad when I was younger, and I know I have not given my mum an easy time, but last night was a wake-up call for me. Again, I am so sorry."

Aaron held out his hand, and Bree shook it, even though it was painful to do so.

"Okay, Aaron, I have this all written down, and when I have typed it up, I will get you to sign it," Sean advised him. "Regarding restitution—either through paying money or by working on the farms—and apologising to the farmers, well, that will be up to the court to decide. But your admission will be put forward to the court for consideration."

Bree thanked Aaron, and wished him the best.

CHAPTER TEN

Sean took Aaron to the holding cell and came back to finish up with Bree, "I will be in touch if there is anything else, but from now on … just behave!"

Bree told Sean she was going to the doctor to see about her hand, and he requested she get a report for him to put with the file.

Bree drove around to the doctor's surgery, unfortunately, he wasn't available, and the receptionist advised her to go to the hospital instead.

So Bree drove to the hospital and waited to see a doctor there. The doctor looked at her injured hand, then with a puzzled look, he commented to Bree, "This is the hand of a bloke who got into a good fight. Have you been fighting?"

"I may have just hit a bloke," she said.

After x-ray's were taken, it was confirmed Bree *had* broken a bone in her hand, and she had to have a plaster cast on it for six weeks. After the cast was applied, Bree took the medical report and dropped it off at the

Chilly police station.

Bree then called around to the produce store and saw Phil. He looked at her, and said, "What have you done? Did it happen last night?"

Bree asked, "What do you mean?"

"It's all over town what you and the blokes did last night. People can't believe that 'quiet Bree' did that. All I can say is, I hope no one tries to take anything from the store when you're here!"

"Well, Phil, I'm going to be in plaster for six weeks, and I am going to be useless in the store. Can I take two weeks off, and then come back to light duties?" Bree asked.

Phil assured Bree, "No worries, you look after yourself. You have plenty of sick leave to cover some time off. If you need anything just yell out."

Bree thanked Phil for his understanding, and was leaving when Olivia came into the store.

"I just heard about last night. Are you okay?" Spotting the plaster cast on Bree's hand, Olivia gasped, "Did you get hurt? Oh no, what happened?"

When Bree could finally get a word in, she answered, "I am okay, but could you call out home this afternoon?" and Olivia said yes, she would.

After her conversation with Olivia, Bree visited Rick at his auto repair shop. "What on earth have you done to yourself?" Rick asked.

"Just a broken bone in my hand from last night. I wanted to know if *you* are okay after everything that happened last night?" she asked.

"I'm fine, I have already given my statement to Sean … and I got put on a warning," Rick replied self-consciously, and just a bit sheepishly.

Bree told Rick to look after himself, and said she was heading home. As Bree was walking out the door Rick called for her to hold on.

"I didn't know you could fight or even get that mad. I'll make sure I never get on *your* wrong side. But are you really okay after last night? You were gunning for somebody!"

Bree assured Rick she was fine, and that she just wanted to go home and rest her hand. She gave Rick a cuddle and headed home, driving cautiously all the way now with her right hand in plaster. It wasn't ideal, but in the country you do what you have to.

At home Cody had helped the tow truck driver recover the blokes' ute, and when the truck had gone Cody fixed the fence so no cattle would escape. While he was fixing the fence, Cody thought to himself that in all the years he had known Bree, he had never seen her so angry, and he had never, ever seen her throw a punch. He had a laugh, and thought to himself, *'Well, that's my girl!'*

Bree arrived home, and when Beth saw the plaster cast on her hand she asked, "Oh no, what happened?"

Bree told her mum how she had gone to the hospital to get it checked, and that an x-ray showed she had broken a bone in her hand, so she had to have the plaster on for six weeks.

Over coffee Bree told Beth and Paul everything that happened at the police station. Then she said she was tired and went to her bedroom for a sleep.

Shortly afterwards Cody arrived back at the house, as he walked in Beth put her finger up to her mouth to say 'quiet', and she steered Cody outside. She told Cody everything Bree had said, particularly about the broken bone in Bree's hand, and how much she was worried about her now.

Cody sat Beth down on one of the outside chairs. "I have never seen her like that and, yes, I was worried, but what has happened has happened. In a few days, I plan to sit down with Bree and talk to her about it. I have a feeling, though, she may get some trouble from the father of one of the blokes."

Cody asked Beth, "Do you know the Brighton's from Huntsville?" Beth nodded. Cody went on, "The main bloke's father is Douglas Brighton Sr., he's a barrister, and he is *not* a nice one! He's managed to have his son, Douglas Jr., cleared of similar charges over in Huntsville a number of times. Beth, we must be prepared for what's to come."

Beth hung her head, deep in thought, and then she looked up. "Cody love, can you help us please? Paul and I don't have any idea of what to do with things like this."

"I was going home anyway to talk to Dad to see what can be done … and if he could help. Dad knows a big-shot lawyer down in Triton." Triton was the capital city of the state, and Beth had never been there.

Beth said, "Thank you, Cody, I don't know what I'm going to do with Bree, and I'm worried that she might be in lot of trouble."

"Mum, the whole district is talking already about what Bree, and us boys, did. They can't believe how she brought those idiots to a stop. But we will take it one day at a time. I will talk to Dad and perhaps see if he can come over and talk to us all about our options." Then Cody added gently, "How's that, okay? Now, you go inside and make yourself a cup of coffee, and I will be back as soon as I can." Cody gave Beth a cuddle and then left to go to home to Aurora Station.

When Bree woke up it was after lunch, and she went out to the kitchen to see her mum. Beth asked Bree if she felt any better.

"Thanks Mum, but the farm won't run itself, so I better go and do something," said Bree.

Beth told Bree that Cody had done everything that needed doing that morning, and he had gone home for something. She offered Bree a coffee and a sandwich.

"Thanks Mum, that would be nice. Yell out when it's

ready, I'm going to sit out on the verandah for a bit."

Taking in the fresh air Bree realised she felt much better after her sleep. Beth came out to the verandah with Bree's coffee and sandwich. "I'm worried you may have gone too far last night, and I'm worried what repercussions may come from it."

* * *

That afternoon at about 3 p.m. Cody and his dad, Thomas, arrived over at the house.

Thomas said, "Hi," to Beth and Paul, and to Bree. He asked if they could talk at the table.

"Cody told me what happened last night, and, Bree, I am glad you're alright—other than your hand, of course. Out of concern for the situation, I contacted my friend, Pat O'Connor. He's one of the top lawyers in Triton." Thomas added, "He says that Douglas Brighton Sr. is one of the most crooked barristers in the district, and he knows he will play dirty. Pat owes me a favour and he has offered his services free of char—." Paul interrupted Thomas, saying they couldn't afford to pay a barrister.

Thomas reassured Paul, saying, "You won't have to pay Pat anything and if, for any reason, there were any fees, I would pay them. Pat has instructed me to tell you *not* to speak to Douglas Brighton, Sr. under any circumstances. If he comes to the house, make sure you have a witness with you, or better still have Cody or Bree record it on their mobile phones." Thomas let this sink in before continuing, "Cody told me that Douglas Brighton Jr. threatened and verbally assaulted Bree. Brighton Jr. told Bree that he was going to come back to finish her … and burn the house down as well."

Beth gasped and put her hands up to her face, and Paul turned to Bree and said angrily, "Brenda, what have you done?!"

Thomas said, "Easy, Paul, hopefully he will never get near the place. Pat is already submitting an application for a private Apprehended Violence Order with the court in Triton. He's requesting that the Brightons are restricted to keep at least five kilometres away from the homestead, and that they are not allowed in Chilly or to contact Bree, other than through her lawyer."

Thomas paused, allowing everyone time to process this information. "Don't worry, if it does go to court, and I dare say it will go to court in Braham, Pat will be with you and the young ones as their solicitor."

Beth said, "Thomas, how can we repay you? We don't have money."

Cody leant forward and said "What about all the home-cooked meals and coffees and love you have both given to me and the boys? Let alone all the conversations, and how many times have I cried on your shoulders?" Beth squeezed Cody's hands, with tears in her eyes. He went on, "Yes, what we did … well … we shouldn't have done it. But the police had done *nothing*, and the livelihood of all farmers here in Chilly, and in Huntsville, was at stake. Plus, I would never, in a blue fit, let Bree go out alone. After this, Sean will have to pick up his act or he will be transferred. If he had done his job properly … well, things would have been different."

Thomas spoke next, "Cody, do you have your mobile phone on you? I take it, Beth, neither you nor Paul own a mobile phone?"

Beth confirmed neither of them had a mobile phone.

"Okay, for the protection of all of you, could Cody move in here? I would feel better if he was here. He can't be a witness to anything because he's already involved, but he would be here for your safety."

Beth spoke up and said, "Yes please, Thomas. Knowing what Douglas Jr. has threatened, it would be best if Cody stayed here."

"I hope you don't mind," said Thomas, "but I phoned Sean and spoke to him on your behalf. We discussed everything, and I advised him that you have a solicitor, and I gave him Pat's contact details. Sean informed me that Douglas Jr. is still on remand in jail and will be until his court appearance. The other blokes have been released with warnings. They had their guns confiscated because they had no gun licences, and they've been told to stay away from here."

Thomas paused to allow the others to speak, but when no one did, he continued on. "One of the blokes,

Aaron, has written a letter to Bree stating he is willing to make restitution for the damages he has caused, and that he is no longer in contact with Douglas Jr."

Beth and Paul both thanked Thomas, and Paul asked, "What about the other farmers? They lost cattle as well, and suffered damage to their farms too."

Thomas informed him that Pat was seeking restitution for the other farmers too. He told them Pat had contacted them individually and instructed them what to do, especially if Douglas Sr. approached them or contacted them in any way.

CHAPTER ELEVEN

It now was about 6 p.m. and the sun was starting to set, when out of nowhere there was a knock on the front door. That was odd, because *no one* knocked on the front door; in the country everyone came to the back door. Beth got up and answered it.

"Good evening, I am wanting to talk to Bree Douglas, is she home?" asked the stranger.

"Who might you be? I don't know you," Beth said, standing with her hands on her hips.

"My name is Douglas Brighton Sr., and I want to talk to Bree about her actions last night."

Thankfully, Thomas was still there and he motioned to Cody to get his mobile phone and put it on 'record'.

Beth came back inside the house and told Bree that Douglas Brighton Sr. was at the door and that he wanted to speak to her. Bree went to the front door, and Thomas stayed out of sight, but he could still see her and hear the conversation.

"I'm Bree Douglas—what do you want?" Bree said

sternly, looking him straight in the eye.

"I wish to talk to you alone, please," said Douglas Sr.

Bree stood her ground with her hands on her hips. "If you have something to say to me you can say it here, and NOW."

Bree's defiance irritated Douglas Sr. "How *dare* you hurt my son!" he thundered. Noticing the plaster cast on Bree's hand he went on, "I can see you were injured too—well, that *is* justice. You and your gunned-up puppy-dogs have some nerve, threatening my son! He was only having fun," Douglas Sr. reasoned.

Cody was furious, he found it hard to sit and listen to Douglas Sr. verbally attacking Bree.

Enraged, Bree took a step towards Douglas Sr. "You are a joke! Your son blatantly verbally abused me, and he entered my property illegally. His 'fun', as you say, has cost me money. He damaged fences and he killed four of my breeding cows, and *then* he threatened to come back to finish me off and burn my family's home down too!"

Bree had not finished with Douglas Sr. "You say your son was only having fun. If this is the way you have raised him then you are an irresponsible father."

Whilst Bree was talking she was gradually inching forward, down the two steps at the front of the house towards Douglas Sr. until they were almost standing nose-to-nose.

Douglas Sr. was taken aback by Bree's determination. "Well … how much is it going to cost for you to drop all charges against my son, and to forget about what he did?" Douglas Brighton Sr. asked.

Bree was beyond angry. She took in a deep breath while looking back at the house, and she could just see Thomas and Cody holding their phones up, and Paul and Beth as well.

Bree whistled for the working dogs, and all three came running to her and sat at her feet.

"I will *not* drop any charges because your son has blatantly broken the law. And the police are laying charges against him as well. As for offering money, hmm … that there is your downfall." Seeing the alarmed look on Douglas Sr.'s face encouraged Bree to continue. "Behind me are two cameras recording our conversation. I will be contacting my solicitor and letting him know exactly what has taken place here this afternoon."

Unable to hold back any longer, Paul was suddenly beside Bree, and he asked her, "You okay?" And then looking directly at Douglas Sr. he asked, "Is there a problem here?"

Pointing towards the gate, and speaking with determination, Bree addressed Douglas Brighton Sr., "You are on private property, and you are an unwelcome guest. Leave now!"

Douglas Sr. looked at them, calculating his options.

"Would $200,000 be enough for you to consider dropping the charges?"

In answer, Bree roared at Douglas Sr., "You are illegally on my property. Leave now and never contact me or my family again, and *never* come back here. You are an uninvited guest, now GET OFF my farm! GET THE HELL OFF!!"

Douglas Sr. tried to negotiate again, but this time Bree ordered menacingly, "You have ONE second to start leaving or these three will help you!" Bree indicated to the dogs, and on cue they growled at Douglas Sr.

Bree and Paul watched Douglas Sr. leave. Paul walked Bree inside and she collapsed onto the lounge. Cody came over to her and cuddled her, and then Bree started sobbing.

Thomas quickly rang Pat and told him what had happened, and he confirmed they had recorded it all on their phones. Pat instructed Thomas, "Email the recordings to me. I will be contacting the police commissioner about Sean as he should have warned Brighton to stay away from Bree and the others. Brighton must be stopped. Did you get his number plate?"

Thomas responded, pleased with himself, "Better than that—I took a photo of his car, and it clearly shows the number plate. I'll email that to you as well." Thomas hung up the phone band sent the files to Pat before returning to Bree and the others.

"Bree, I am so proud of you the way you handled

Brighton Sr.—you did so well! I have just spoken to Pat, and he thinks you did well too, and he hopes you're okay," said Thomas. "Pat is also going to be dealing with Sean's superiors after what Brighton has done because—I bet you—he has offered to buy Sean's silence. Worst thing for Brighton Sr. is we got him on video, and he probably won't be a practising barrister for too much longer; Pat is dealing with that."

Bree hugged Cody, "What have I done?!" she asked. She was a strong lady, but after the confrontation with Douglas Brighton Sr., the tears and sobs continued, and Bree crumpled into Cody's arms. The aggression from Douglas Sr. had triggered a memory of Bob's attack on her at the rodeo last year, and she was experiencing a mental breakdown. Thomas grabbed his mobile phone and called the local doctor to immediately come out to The Flats to attend to her.

While this was happening Olivia arrived, and Beth went outside to her and told her what had just happened. She also explained that Bree was struggling with the stress from it all, and Olivia asked if she could do anything to help. Beth pulled her aside and said "Watch your back, and talk to the other boys and tell them to NOT to talk to Douglas Brighton Sr."

Olivia replied, "Don't worry, I'll talk to the others, and anyone else who has been affected. Is it okay if they want to call out here and check on Bree? We all love her and care about her." Beth said, "Of course, that would be lovely, but make sure they phone me first to see if Bree is up to having visitors. Oh, and Cody is staying here for our protection until things are sorted out." Olivia hugged Beth and reminded her that she was always there for Bree.

Understanding that now was not the time to catch up with Bree, Olivia got back into her car and headed into town to see the others. She would phone Beth in the evening to get a progress report on how her friend was recovering.

* * *

Days went by, and Douglas Sr. was doing the rounds of the other farmers who had been targeted by Douglas Jr. Each time he was met with, "Get out and don't come back!"

Sean was subdued and quiet because his boss from Braham had come down to Chilly to oversee the case.

It was now early September, and the trial was due to commence over in Braham. Unusually, the two separate, but related, cases—the damage caused by Douglas Jr. and his crew, and the bribery allegation against Douglas Sr.—were going to be prosecuted under the same trial. This was due to the looming retirement of the only circuit judge for their district.

As the replacing judge was unable to commence for many months—due to an accident which meant he would be incapacitated—the Brightons' cases had been moved forward so that the current judge could preside over them. This also meant that sentencing and costs directions would be determined at the time of the trial.

The retiring judge was well known for his no-nonsense stance, and was generally considered 'tough but fair'. He was worn down by his workload and the increasing amount of entitled young men who appeared before him who showed no regard for the rights of others, or their property.

Over his many decades as a judge he had developed a strong dislike of the privileged few who seemed to escape paying for the consequences of their actions. Slick barristers like Douglas Brighton Sr. were part of the problem, as he saw it.

As this was going to be the last trial before his retirement he was in no mood to humour the likes of Douglas Brighton Sr. or his delinquent son! He was keen to get this trial over and done with.

Bree, Cody and the boys had to attend court in Braham to answer for using firearms and detaining the hell-raisers, so Paul, Beth, and Thomas went with them. Thomas paid for them all to stay in the motel in town—not the 'usual one'—as they called it, but the 'fancy motel'. Thomas had arranged for two farm-hands to stay at Paul's and Beth's farm, The Flats, and take care of it while they were away in Braham.

Thomas met Pat in the bar of the motel that afternoon. "Hi, Thomas, how are you going? How is Bree and her family?" Pat asked his friend.

Thomas looked serious as he replied, "Bree is a strong lady, but … well, she has had a few days where she has cried, and everything was getting to her. She keeps saying that she is frightened that Douglas Jr. will be cleared of the charges and then he will come for her and burn the house down."

Pat was clearly concerned by this, and Thomas continued on, "After Douglas Sr. was at the house Bree came inside and collapsed in tears. Cody and I were really worried about her, and I called our doctor out to attend to her. I am concerned for Bree; seeing Douglas Jr. at the trial could trigger another breakdown, and I dare say his mouth will be going as well! Cody won't leave Bree's side, as he is worried about her too."

Pat said to him, "When is that boy going to put a ring on Bree's finger? Everyone can see how much he cares for her." Pat added, "Okay, Bree's condition is noted for court. Do you think she can cope with it?"

Thomas replied, "She will have to, and I will make sure that she and her family get whatever help they need to get through this."

Thomas spoke to Pat at length about Paul's heart condition and how the farm was Bree's, but for the finalising the paperwork. He told Pat about how committed Bree was to the farm, and how her two brothers wanted nothing to do with it. He also reminded Pat that Sean was a disappointment as a local police officer, as it was Bree who found out all the information about the troublemakers and hatched a plan to catch them when Sean had done nothing.

Pat said, "That's what I wondered from the start, why Sean didn't do his job has got me, but he is going to pay for his lack of investigation. A citizen shouldn't have to take law enforcement into their own hands to get justice—if you call it that. I figured that Bree was very protective of the farm for a reason, and don't worry, if Paul wants, I can draw up the papers for the farm transfer for him from here." Pat paused to take a sip of his drink. "Because of Douglas Sr.'s actions and the video you sent me, he is probably going to be struck off so he will no longer be able to practise as a barrister, he may even face jail time."

Thomas said, "Pat, how can I ever repay you for all you are doing? Bree means so much to me. She's the daughter I always wanted, and … well, Paul and Beth and I are hoping that Cody gets his act together and puts a ring on Bree's finger—sooner rather than later. I worry about Paul, though. He can't do the jobs he used to do because of his heart condition, and there are days when he gets … 'upset', let's say. Paul's cardiac specialist has said he mustn't have any stress."

Thomas thought for a moment, and asked Pat, "Court starts tomorrow at 9 a.m., and after that visit from Douglas Sr. is there any way that we can separate the Brightons from Bree and the others when she gives evidence? I daresay she could get upset, so would it be possible for Beth and Cody to be with her?"

Pat told Thomas not to worry, he was also concerned about Bree, so he would sort something out. He also knew the circuit judge who would be presiding over the case, in fact they had studied law together. The judge was not afraid of handing out tough sentences, especially as he was at the end of his career. Pat knew, also, that there was history between the judge and the Brighton family.

That night they all had dinner together and Pat went through what they should expect, and he also gave them an outline of court proceedings. He suggested they should all have an early night as tomorrow would be a tough day.

CHAPTER TWELVE

The next morning Bree, Cody, Beth, Paul, Thomas, and the boys and their families all went into the courtroom together. Pat checked with Bree that she was alright, and then asked Beth and Cody to sit each side of her.

The trial commenced and Douglas Jr. was brought in to the courtroom, and he began mouthing-off at Bree straight away. His barrister—who was one of his father's questionable associates—tried to shut him up, but he could not control him, and knew he could not win a case with a client like that. When the judge entered the courtroom Douglas Jr. was still going.

"Counsel, please quieten your client or I will have him removed, *and* I will charge him with contempt of court," instructed the judge.

Douglas Sr. reached forward from the row behind and told Douglas Jr. to stop and be quiet. As the trial progressed it came time for Bree to take the witness stand. Pat spoke to the judge and he agreed that, rather than entering the witness box, Bree could give her evidence from the table while standing, with her mother and

Cody sitting either side of her. Before Bree could speak, Douglas Jr. was again mouthing-off, but this time he stood up and screamed, "You rotten bitch! I will get you for this — you are dead!"

Cody jumped to his feet, but Pat pushed him down in his seat, and Thomas put a hand on his shoulder and whispered, "Stay son, wait for it."

Beth stood up and hugged Bree, and the judge asked if Bree was alright to continue. Beth replied that Bree wasn't able to continue because of Douglas Jr.'s malicious outburst.

Douglas Jr. was still going off and Douglas Sr. was trying to calm him down, but Junior just shrugged him off. The judge stood up and banged his gavel down hard on the block.

The judge turned to Bree and said, "Miss Douglas, You may sit down now." Bree was tearful, and as she sat down Cody put his arms protectively around her and gently wiped the tears from her face.

The judge asked the sergeant, "Please bring Douglas Brighton Jr. down in front of the bench. And both counsels — please come forward." Two sergeants moved to either side of Douglas Jr. and physically escorted him to the front of the bench.

Douglas Jr. was ranting again as he was being escorted, when the judge erupted. He could stand no more of this behaviour and he was ready to throw the book at Douglas Brighton Jr. "Enough! I said enough!

You are a disgrace — you have disgraced the court, and I will *not* stand for your outbursts. I fine you $10,000 for contempt of court. Your behaviour leaves me no other option than to sentence you here and now.

"Douglas Brighton Jr, I hereby sentence you to incarceration on *The Island* for thirty years with hard labour, and no eligibility for parole. You are violent, and you are unpredictable, thus you are a danger to society. Additionally you will pay all court costs for both parties, *and* you will give the farmers, whose livestock and property you have attacked in the Chilly and Huntsville areas, restoration for all the damage that you have inflicted on them.

"Furthermore, I make an order that you have no contact with any of the parties involved in this case, in any shape or form, for the rest of your life." Then the judged turned to the sergeant, "Sergeant, does this courthouse have a dual chain restraint?" The sergeant confirmed that they did.

"Please bring a new one to the court room," requested the judge.

As the name suggested, *The Island* was a jail situated on an island offshore from Triton. It was a maximum-security prison for mentally disturbed offenders and violent offenders who had been denied parole.

Douglas Brighton Sr. was talking to the barrister acting for him and his son, when the judge asked if there was a problem. The counsel replied, "No, your Honour."

The sergeant returned with the new shackles and put the restraints on Douglas Jr.

The judge said "Sergeant, please give me the key so that I can personally check that the restraint is locked properly." Once the judge was satisfied with the integrity of the locks, two sergeants escorted Douglas Jr. back to the holding cell.

Then, one by one, the judge called forward three of the blokes who had been arrested with Douglas Brighton Jr. They each received a $5,000 fine, a five-year good behaviour bond, and were ordered to pay $1,000 restitution to the farmers who had lost cattle.

The judge then called Aaron James forward, "Mr James, I understand that you were the first to give up your rifle on the night in question, and that you have already apologised to Ms Douglas. In your signed confession you said you are willing to pay back to each farmer the cost of the damage you have caused. I understand you have limited financial resources, but you are willing to work on each farm to pay restitution. Is that right?"

Aaron James answered the judge, "Yes sir, I am willing to work on all the farms if the farmers will allow it. I have seen the error of my ways and wish to change."

The judge said "I have read your confession to Ms Douglas, that was documented by the police sergeant at Chilly, and I accept that you have realised your wrongdoings. My sentencing to you is as follows. You are to work on each farm where you killed cattle and damaged property, I also fine you $1,000, and place you on a two-year good behaviour bond. If you appear in court within those two years, you will be imprisoned for five years. Do you understand, Mr James?

Aaron answered, "Yes, Your Honour, and thank you."

Pat asked the judge for a fifteen-minute recess, in view of the outbursts from Douglas Jr., which had been extremely upsetting for Bree.

The judge agreed and called a fifteen-minute recess, and then added, "After that last outburst from Mr Douglas Brighton Jr. I know I could certainly do with a coffee!" The judge's comment gave rise to some chuckles from the gallery.

Thomas asked Bree if she was alright, and if she needed to see a doctor. Bree assured Thomas she was fine now, but she wanted to leave the courtroom to get some fresh air and a drink. Pat had already organised a designated room for them where they all could have a break and a drink in privacy.

On the way to the break-room Beth noticed the media gathering outside. Pat looked at Thomas and said, "I'm sorry about this, but I didn't tell you all because you have enough to deal with. Unfortunately, the case has attracted media attention because of Brighton and his son. Apparently, Brighton Sr. went directly to the media saying Bree targeted his son because *he* refused her affections."

"What the hell?!" exclaimed Cody. "In a million years she wouldn't go for a low life like him!"

Thomas said, "Cool down, son, we all know that. But when we go back in there you're going to hear things you don't agree with, and you're going to have to keep it together—otherwise you're going to end up like Brighton Jr."

Cody took Beth aside and quietly said, "We should still sit either side of Bree when we go back to the courtroom, she needs our support even more now, thanks to the media!" Beth reached up and cradled Cody's face in her hands, "Son, we will stay with Bree for sure, but listen to your father, please." Cody gave Beth a hug and walked over to Bree and put a protective arm around her shoulder. The sergeant knocked on the half-open door and told them court was back in session, so they all headed for the courtroom.

In court Pat stood up and gave an outline of Douglas Sr.'s unwelcome visit to The Flats. He emphasised how traumatising and triggering the exchange had been for Bree, and the toll that the subsequent court case was taking on her.

The judge agreed to this, but the opposing counsel objected. In true 'country court' style, the judge told him to shut up and sit down.

Bree gave her evidence, and the video of Douglas Sr.'s attempt to bribe her was played. After giving her evidence the judge thanked Bree, and told her that she could sit down now.

The judge said quickly, "Counsellor, I take it that Douglas Brighton Sr. is in court?"

"Yes, Your Honour," replied the defence counsel.

"Douglas Brighton Sr., please stand, and come to the front of the courtroom," requested the judge. When Bree saw Douglas Brighton Sr. come forward she leant closer to Cody.

"Mr Brighton, you are a member of the bar are you not?' asked the judge.

"Yes, your Honour, I am, and I have been for thirty years now."

The judge leaned on the bench, looking over the top of his glasses at Brighton Sr. and reprimanded him. "I have never been so disgusted in a member of the bar than I am today. You not only harassed this young woman, but you also threatened her, and I have been reliably informed you contacted the media and told them a whole bunch of lies."

Brighton Sr.'s barrister jumped to his feet, but before he could say a word the judge picked up a thick folder and waved it at Douglas Brighton Sr.

"I have gone back through your cases for the last year, and I am totally disgusted. This morning I contacted the bar association and I told them what you have been up to. I have sent them copies of your cases for the last year, and they are now under review. Considering the evidence that has been given, I find you guilty of extortion and fraudulent misrepresentation.

"I am going to recommend to the bar association to have you struck off! I am also sentencing you to ten years in the jail in Triton. NO Parole. Sergeant take him out of my sight."

The judge then called Josh, Rick, Nick, BJ, and Cody to stand before the court.

"To each of you I will say this: I have reviewed the evidence and the statements you gave to the police following the incident in question. Your admissions of guilt and your remorse for your actions are duly noted. It was irresponsible of you to do what you did in ambushing the five trespassers; however, I know you all have learnt a valuable lesson from this. I hereby place each of you on a three-year good behaviour bond, and I never want to hear about any of you being in a courtroom in the next three years." The judge dismissed the boys and they returned to their seats.

The judge then called Bree to stand before the court and she stood up shakily with Cody beside her.

"Brenda, or Bree?" asked the judge.

"Bree please, Your Honour," she replied.

"Young lady, what you did was irresponsible, and to involve your friends was doubly irresponsible. I understand you were protecting your farm, but the way you went about it was unlawful and reckless. You are fortunate that you and your friends weren't shot. I can see that these events have taken an emotional strain on you, and that the plaster cast on your hand has taught you a worthwhile lesson about fist-fighting."

The judge asked if Bree had anything she wanted to say to the court. Bree said, "Your Honour, I know what I did was irresponsible and I should never have involved my friends. Yes, I should also never have used my fists, but as a woman it hurt being called those names, and I was defending myself and the farm. I wish to apologise to Rick, Nick, Josh, BJ, and Cody for putting them in a dangerous position, and I regret ever having involved them. Thank you, Your Honour."

The judge responded, "You are genuinely remorseful, I can see that, and I am sorry you felt you had to take the law into your own hands. Taking everything into consideration, I am placing you on a five-year good behaviour bond. However, I will not be suspending your firearms license as you require it to run your farm. I wish you a speedy recovery from this ordeal."

Pat stood up and asked permission to speak. "Your Honour, because of Mr Douglas Brighton Sr.'s actions there is a media circus at the front of the building. I would prefer that my clients—particularly, Ms Douglas—be spared from any unnecessary attention from the media."

The judge said, "Sergeant, I want you to go and instruct the media to relocate to the central town park where they will be given a media statement in due course. If anyone doesn't go—lock them up!"

The judge turned to the courtroom in general and said, "Ms Douglas has written a statement, which she has asked to be read out in court." Facing Cody, Rick, Nick, Josh, and BJ, the judge instructed them, "Gentlemen, please stand."

The court clerk read the statement aloud, "Guys, I am deeply sorry for getting you all into trouble. It was selfish to ask for your help in that stupid action. I hope you can all forgive me, but I understand if you don't want anything to do with me ever again. I am so sorry—Bree."

Nick asked the judge if he could speak. "Yes, son, state your full name," replied the judge.

"My name is Nick Holmes, Your Honour."

Nick turned towards Bree. "Bree, we all went to school together so we have known each other for a long time now. We have all been there for one another through the good and the bad. I personally don't hold a grudge against you, and I could never have let you deal with Douglas Jr. and 'friends' on your own. You mean the world to us," he said. The judge addressed Bree, "Ms Douglas, you are a fortunate young woman to have forgiving friends like this young man."

The judge then declared that the trial was concluded, and the court was dismissed.

CHAPTER THIRTEEN

Back at the motel it was time to debrief, and for coffee all round. Thomas and Cody had a suite consisting of two bedrooms, a bathroom, a kitchenette, a dining area, and a spacious living room. Everyone met back at Thomas's and Cody's suite to talk over the day's events and to catch their breath.

Still standing, Pat addressed the group. "While we have everyone here, I think we should take the opportunity to execute the documents I have prepared to transfer ownership of The Flats from Paul and Beth over to Bree. Paul, Beth, and Bree, you will need to sign these documents, of course, and I will need three witnesses to witness each signatory. Perhaps, Thomas, Cody and Nick could do that?"

The signatories and the witnesses gathered around the dining table. Pat read the documents out aloud so that Paul, Beth and Bree were clear on their contents. As intended, the documents transferred ownership of the property to Bree, and acknowledged that Paul and Beth would remain as her financial backers in running the farm business, and retain a small monetary interest in the enterprise. Once everything had been signed and checked there was a feeling of relief and celebration in the room. Backs were slapped, hands were shaken, and hugs given and received. Paul thanked Pat and Thomas for their generosity in arranging the transfer, and told them he did not know what he would do without their help.

Even though it had ended well, the events of the day had exhausted Bree, physically, mentally, and emotionally. She admitted that she was worn out and said that she was going to lie down, and Cody went to be with her.

As they walked to the suite she was sharing with Paul and Beth, Bree asked Cody, "Why do you still want anything to do with me? I got you and the others in *so* much trouble!"

Cody replied, "You never have to worry about that, we all love you and care about you. We could not have let you go out by yourself to deal with Douglas Jr. and his 'friends'. Plus, Olivia, Jenny, and Charlie have been ringing wanting to know how you are—they are all worried about you."

Bree collapsed on to her bed and Cody gently placed a blanket around her and told her to get some rest. She reached for his arm, "Please stay with me until I go to sleep." And with that, Cody lay on the bed cuddling her until she drifted off to sleep.

Cody then went back his suite to have a coffee with the others when there was a knock on the door. Thomas answered it, to find Rick was standing there. Rick had excused himself earlier and had gone to the room he was sharing with Nick, Josh, and BJ to check in on his business by phone. He asked if he could talk to Pat for a moment. "Pat, I would like to thank you for everything you have done today. I'm still really worried about Bree though," Rick said.

Pat said, "It's fine, I was happy to be of help, and I am glad the courts dealt with the Brightons. Yes, it has been an ordeal for Bree, but I will make sure she has whatever help is needed."

"Pat, what do I do if Sean starts harassing us?" Rick asked. "I'm a mechanic and Nick is a carpenter, and we don't need our businesses affected by Sean. We're both worried."

Pat pulled a business card out of his wallet and handed it to Rick, "If you have any trouble you contact me, okay? But by the time you all get back to Chilly I think Sean will have either been transferred, *or* he will have a superior at the station for a length of time." Pat paused, and then continued, "He will receive some type of disciplinary action because of his sloppy policing, and his failure to keep the community safe. I wish you all the best, Rick, and the same to the others, too."

Rick said goodbye to everyone and told them he would catch up with them at home, and with that he and the rest of the blokes departed for the drive home to Chilly.

Beth said she was exhausted and that she was going for a rest, and then Paul said he was feeling weary and he would join her too. So the two of them left and headed for their suite.

Thomas, Pat, and Cody had ordered room service, and they now sat drinking their coffee and eating in comfortable silence for a few minutes.

Then Pat turned to Cody and said, "Son, you have feelings for Bree, don't you?"

Cody responded, "Yes, Pat, I love her. It's killing me seeing her in so much pain, and I can't do anything to take it away."

"Well, son, do you want to marry her?"

"I would marry Bree tomorrow if I could, but she had a terrible break up with a bloke—if you can call him that—over a year ago, and I don't want to push her."

"Have you made your feelings known to her?"

"Yes, Bree knows that I have strong feelings for her, and that I will always protect her," said Cody.

"Well, put a ring on that finger as soon as you can. You will never find another woman like Bree."

The three men had finished their meals, so Pat said his goodbyes to Thomas and Cody, and reminded them that if they needed anything they should contact him.

The next day the last of them all headed home: Cody and Bree drove together, and Thomas drove Beth and Paul in his car.

On the way home, Cody asked Bree if she was okay. "I will be. Only wish I had not let my temper get the better of me. I just want to go home and get stuck into work on the farm."

Cody smiled at her and suggested, "You can't do much with that plaster on your arm, but for now why don't you slide over here and put the middle seatbelt on, rest against me and have a sleep."

Bree didn't have the energy to argue. She was so tired. She noticed Cody was wearing the aftershave she loved. Bree leant against Cody and rested her plastered hand on his thigh.

After about two hours, Cody pulled into The Flats. Bree was still asleep, so he lifted her out of the ute and headed for the backdoor of the homestead. Before he reached it the door opened and Terry—one of the farmhands who was looking after the farm while they were at the trial—let Cody go through with Bree still in his arms.

Thomas, Beth, and Paul arrived soon afterwards. Thomas thanked Terry for looking after the farm and asked if there had been any problems.

"No, I went into town for some supplies this morning, and the court case and all the stuff with Brightons were what everyone was talking about." Terry added with a smile, "Oh, Sean has been transferred, and we have *two* new police officers now. They did call here at the farm, but I told them I was only looking after the place until you all got back. So, I dare say, expect a visit from the police."

Beth acknowledged that she was worried about how Bree would cope with *more* contact with the police, especially at home. Thomas said he would go into town and talk to the police to see what they wanted.

Thomas then said goodbye to Cody and added, "Any trouble—ring me asap." He gave Beth a cuddle, and Paul put his hand out to shake Thomas's hand.

Terry said his goodbyes too, and then Paul, Beth, and Cody all said coffee was needed.

* * *

A few days later Bree came to Cody and asked, "Can you come into town with me please? I want to get some things from the produce store for the cattle."

Cody checked with Beth to see if she wanted anything from town while they were there.

"Hang on, I will get you some money. I need bread, coffee, and a few other things. I'll ring Ruth at the grocery store and put my order in," Beth answered.

When Bree and Cody reached the produce store they spoke to Phil.

"Hi, Phil, do you have any worm and tick spray for my

cattle? And I'll need some ear tags for the calves as well," said Bree.

Phil responded as he put Bree's order together, "You can't do much with your arm in plaster, but yes, here we go. Is that all you need today? When you are ready to come back to work, give me a call. Remember, the job is yours and no one else's."

"Thanks, Phil, for everything. I'll give you a call in about two weeks. Is that okay?" asked Bree.

"Yes, Bree, that's fine. If you need anything else in the meantime, just yell out."

Cody and Bree then headed to the grocery store, where Ruth had already packed up Beth's order.

"Hi, you two, how are you both going now?" asked Ruth, smiling. "Here's Beth's order, and could you give her this letter? It's only the minutes of the last CWA meeting."

With all their jobs completed, Cody and Bree headed home. On the trip back Cody reached over and gently took Bree's plastered hand in his and held it. It felt good, and Cody noticed Bree was getting better after all that had happened, but it would still be a little while yet before she was completely recovered.

* * *

Cody thought it was time for all of them to get together again … maybe even for a weekend away. He would contact the others.

A week later Cody ran into Rick and Nick, and suggested a weekend away after all that everyone had been through with the Brightons.

Nick and Rick said, yes, that would be great. Nick offered to get onto Josh and BJ, and then he would let Cody know if they were interested.

* * *

A few weeks later Paul opened the mail to find a cheque for $3,000 from Brighton Sr. for the damage to the fences and for the cows that had been killed. They were surprised as they all thought Brighton would never pay the restitution ordered by the court.

Paul rang Thomas to tell him the good news, and Thomas informed Paul that Brighton Sr.'s marriage had broken down and their house in Huntsville had been sold. The other farmers who had been victims of Douglas Brighton Jr. also received cheques as restitution. Thomas asked Paul how Bree was doing now and if there was anything he could help with.

Paul answered, "Bree is doing as well as can be expected, it is just going to take time. And thanks for the offer of help, but everything is fine."

It was now late September so Bree and Cody went into Chilly for her plaster cast to be removed from her hand and wrist. It was replaced with a removable wrist splint which was more comfortable, and allowed Bree more movement of her wrist. The break was still not fully healed, so she would still have to be careful with it for a few weeks yet.

Bree felt better after the heavy plaster cast had been cut off. She was told to do hand exercises and to rub skin cream into her hand and arm as the skin had dried out from being in the plaster.

Over the next few weeks Cody took Bree out for drives to see Rick, Nick, and Josh. BJ had moved to Braham for work, so unfortunately the weekend away that Cody wanted them all to go on didn't eventuate.

Olivia had organised to take Bree to a spa in Braham to have her nails done and her hair shampooed and styled. After that Olivia was going to take Bree shopping to buy her a new dress.

Bree agreed—even though there was work to be done—but she thought 'why not?' after everything she had been through recently.

Olivia picked Bree up and they headed to the spa. Bree wasn't sure what style to have her hair cut in, so she asked Olivia for her opinion.

"I don't know which cut or colour suits me, do you have any suggestions?" she asked Olivia.

"I have always been jealous of your long blonde hair, so I wouldn't get a full colour, maybe just some highlights. I definitely don't think you should have it cut short. I would get it trimmed and maybe even styled a bit," Olivia answered truthfully. "You look so beautiful with your long hair. If I let you get it cut off Cody would lose his head at me! Gee, I would surely be in the bad books."

So Bree had her hair trimmed and styled, and some highlights put through as well. She really enjoyed the head massage from the hairdresser when she was having her hair shampooed.

With her hair done, it was time for a manicure and then a pedicure.

Olivia said to Bree, "I know you work hard on the farm, and you don't go for getting your nails done, so I hope you enjoy this. If you have any questions about anything just ask me."

Bree thought, *'This is not me, but I am enjoying it.'*

After her nails were shaped and painted with coloured nail polish, the next thing was makeup. Bree hardly ever wore makeup, so she asked for Olivia to help her.

Olivia replied thoughtfully, "I think just go for something natural — nothing like I do, that's not you. But if you would like, we could get it done a *little bit more* than natural. You have great cheekbones and your blue eyes … oh, we can really make your eyes stand out. Remember the rodeo ball? You looked beautiful and you didn't have much makeup on then."

Again, Bree thought 'why not?', so she said, "Okay!" Having her makeup done was strange to her, but she was loving the attention, and she was learning in case she had to do her makeup by herself in future.

After the makeup session Olivia suggested, "How about we get something to eat?"

"I'm thirsty, and a sandwich would be great," replied Bree. Olivia knew of a great coffee shop, so they headed there. Bree enjoyed the hot coffee and the tasty sandwich too.

"Thank you for all of this, Olivia, it means a lot to me. After the last few months this is exactly what I needed," said Bree.

Olivia laughed to herself — if Bree only knew why this was all happening!

Cody had asked Olivia to help him, as he had a surprise for Bree. He had enlisted Beth's help to decorate the shed with fairy lights, and to cook them a romantic dinner. Then Cody hooked up the Wi-Fi speaker to his phone so that he and Bree could dance.

Olivia said to Bree, "There's a nice dress shop just down the road … let's go and get evening dresses for the both of us."

Bree thought, *'Evening dress? Hmm … what's going on here?'* So she asked Olivia, "Why an evening dress?"

Olivia answered casually, "Well, I need one for next month, and I just thought you would like one too."

At the dress shop Bree looked at the prices and said to Olivia, "I can't afford anything here!"

Olivia said, "My treat. After everything that's happened I want to see the old Bree: happy and smiling and laughing. You've had fun today?"

"Yes, I have had fun! You know that I don't normally do these things, like we have today."

Olivia picked up a romantic full-length black evening gown from the rack. Sheer black chiffon was layered over cream silk, and it was decorated with appliqued black lace across the bodice, forming delicate cap sleeves, and trailing down on to the full skirt. The dress had a v-neckline and was sheer to the nipped-in waist at the back.

"Every girl needs a special black dress," reasoned Olivia. "Hey, why don't you try this one on?"

"Hmm … that dress is not really me," said Bree, unconvinced.

"Try it on, just for a laugh then," Olivia said persuasively.

"Okay … " said Bree, and she went to the dressing room to try the dress on. When Bree walked out of the fitting room, Olivia sat down with her mouth open.

"Does it look that bad?" Bree asked miserably.

Olivia exclaimed "You look so beautiful — but for the boots!"

Bree then looked at herself in the mirror. The dress fitted her like a glove, and the chiffon skirt was just sheer enough so the shape of her long, slender legs could be glimpsed through the fabric.

'Oh my, this dress looks gorgeous. Cody would love this on me. He would be open-mouthed, unable to talk.'

Little did Bree know it, but Olivia had taken a photo of her on her phone and sent it to Cody. Cody answered back, 'You look after my girl.'

After some persuasion Olivia convinced Bree to say 'yes to the dress'.

Olivia suggested that the gorgeous stiletto-heeled shoes Bree had worn to the rodeo ball would be perfect for this dress too, and Bree agreed with her. So with everything done, they left Braham and headed home.

CHAPTER FOURTEEN

Olivia and Bree arrived back at The Flats, and Beth said "Oh, don't you look beautiful, sweetheart!" when the girls entered the kitchen.

Cody came in and stopped in his tracks. His mouth hit the floor, and he couldn't speak. *'Is this my Bree?* he thought, *'She is gorgeous!'*

Bree wasn't used to the attention, so she was feeling embarrassed.

Olivia said, "Oh, you want to see her new dress. It's an evening gown, like nothing else she has in her wardrobe!" Olivia secretly winked at Cody as she said this, knowing full well that he had already seen the sneaky photo that she had taken of Bree trying the dress on in the shop.

Beth was busy cooking when Bree asked what was for dinner. With that, Cody finally found his voice, "I have a surprise for you. You need to put on your new dress and be ready in half an hour. I'm not telling you anything more."

Bree looked at him curiously, and Beth and Olivia were grinning.

"So, are you both in on this surprise?" Bree asked.

They couldn't stay quiet any longer. Olivia said, "Yes we are, and don't think badly about it. You just wait until tonight. Now come on, we must get you ready!"

Bree asked them, "Where am I going, what's on?" But all her questions went unanswered.

Half an hour later and Cody was in the kitchen in a suit and tie. He was freshly shaved and smelling of Bree's favourite aftershave.

When Bree entered the room Cody sat down quickly, Beth turned around and gasped, and Olivia was smiling. Bree couldn't work out why everyone was acting like they were. When she turned to look in the mirror in the lounge room even she was shocked. Shocked in a good way at how beautiful she looked.

Bree looked at Cody and a tear slid down her face. Cody asked her, "What's the matter?"

"You look so handsome in your suit," she said. "I've never seen you look so hot!

Olivia pulled out her phone and said, "Smile!" Cody put an arm around Bree and they beamed a dazzling smile for the photo.

Cody said, "Now, Bree, you must keep your eyes shut—promise?

"Okay, but you will have to guide me," said Bree.

Cody helped Bree and her evening gown into his ute, and he drove to the shed. He said, "Stay in the ute, and no peeking!" and with that he went into the shed and turned the lights on. Cody helped Bree from the ute and walked her to the front door of the shed.

"Okay, you can open your eyes now."

Bree couldn't believe her eyes! Fairy lights twinkled throughout the shed, and candles flickered lightly on a small table that was decorated with roses.

Bree whispered, "Did you do all this today for me?"

Cody turned and faced her, "I did. First, there is something I need to do," and with that he pulled her into a tight embrace with their bodies pressed against each other and he gave her a long, passionate kiss.

"I have been wanting to do that since you came home with Olivia," he said looking lovingly into her eyes.

Cody escorted her into the shed so she could see more. His hand was in the centre of her back, feeling the warmth of her bare skin. He was still amazed at how beautiful the dress looked on her.

He pulled out a chair for Bree to sit on, poured her a glass of champagne, and said dinner would arrive soon. They talked easily together, small talk to start with, but then they also reaffirmed their feelings for one another. Bree reminded Cody that they had not watched the sunset for a long time, and she missed it.

"I promise to see many sunsets with you," he said.

With that, Beth and Olivia arrived with their special dinner: delicious roast beef and vegetables, with pan-made gravy, and a home-baked dinner bun.

Bree was loving her time with Cody, and she was so proud of him that he had gone to so much effort to make this night special. After dinner, he put on the music and asked Bree if she would like to dance. Cody helped her up from her chair, and he led her into the middle of the shed.

Olivia and Beth were hidden from Cody and Bree, and they couldn't help but take a few sneaky-peek photos of the two of them. When they turned away they giggled to themselves.

Olivia whispered, "I never thought Cody was a romantic, but it's obvious that he really loves Bree." Beth agreed with Olivia, and she had tears in her eyes.

Cody held Bree tight against him, and he could feel her slim body against his. Because of the neckline of Bree's dress he could see her small, firm, round breasts; he knew he had to say something … but when?

He was enjoying the feeling of holding her in his arms, when Bree said softly, "I don't know what I would do without you, Cody. You care so much about me, and you do *so* much for me … just look at tonight. I'm so lucky to have you in my life."

"I'm a lucky man to have such a beautiful woman in

my life, and I think you know my feelings for you too."

They danced for what seemed liked hours until Cody asked Bree if she would like a drink. Bree said that she would, and they walked over to the bar Cody had made for them. He gave her a glass of champagne and then he said, "I have another surprise for you, come with me."

He led her to the back of the shed and he opened the back door to show her a bench seat he had made out of hay bales covered with a blanket. They sat down on it and she said she had missed looking at the stars too, just like she had missed the sunsets. Cody took off his suit coat and put it around her shoulders.

"Bree, I have something to ask you. You know I love you so much," Cody said meaningfully, holding her tight to his body.

She replied, "I know, and I'm so thankful for that and everything you do for me."

"You are so attractive, *so* beautiful, and you know how I feel about you and what I must want," Cody said quietly and nervously.

Bree held his face in her hands and said, "I know — soon, okay?"

He held his excitement in. This was something he had wanted for so long.

Time got away from them, sitting snuggled together, looking up at the night sky with all the stars flickering.

Then Cody suggested it was time for them to head back to the house as it was past midnight. As they left the shed, all the candles were blown out, the lights were turned off, and the shed locked up. Cody gave Bree a long kiss and cuddle goodnight.

Bree had the best sleep she'd had in a long time. She missed Cody cuddling her to sleep, but she knew that in time he would cuddle her to sleep every night.

The next morning both Bree and Cody got up early and went into the kitchen. Being early risers, Beth was already in there busy making breakfast, and Paul was sitting at the table enjoying his first coffee of the day.

"Morning, you two, did you have a good night last night?" Beth asked.

Bree and Cody couldn't stop smiling. "Okay, spill it, I can see you two are both grinning like Cheshire Cats," teased Beth.

"Nothing to spill Mum, we just had a good night," Bree said.

"Hey, Dad … if we can talk about the farm … Cody and I are going to start mustering up the cattle to dip and worm them. I have the book of ear tags, and I also got some for all the new calves. If you want to come down to the new stockyards and mark off the ear tag numbers that would really help us," Bree said. "I will take the horses down, and Cody is going to bring everything else we need down in his ute."

Paul said he would be happy to help, and he would come down to the stockyards after his breakfast.

Cody said, "Oh, Dad, I have a surprise for you in the shed. I bought a second-hand farm buggy — you know, an ATV — to help you to get around the farm easier."

Paul beamed, and Bree said, "Dad, that's great! You won't be so housebound now, but you still have to be careful not to overdo things, okay?"

After breakfast Bree and Cody headed for the shed to get the horses and all the gear needed to do the worming and tagging.

Bree enjoyed riding Hayson again, and she was also leading Banjo down to the stockyards while Cody followed in his ute. *'Time to start work,'* Bree thought, and she and Hayson started out to muster up the cattle.

* * *

Back at the homestead Beth said to her husband, "At last they are out of here. I have to ring Thomas and fill him in on last night — I dare say he will be happy."

Thomas picked up the call on the third ring. "Good morning, Thomas, how are you?" Beth asked.

"Hi, Beth, I'm well thanks, how is everything on the farm?" Thomas enquired.

"Are you sitting down? Last night — well it started yesterday … Cody got Olivia to take Bree to Braham and they went to a spa where Bree had her hair cut and some highlights put through, and then she had a man-icure and a pedicure, and *then* they went shopping and Olivia bought Bree a new dress with money Cody had given her. Oh, boy, you should see how beautiful Bree looked!" Beth stopped briefly to take a breath before continuing, "And all the while Cody was doing up the shed for a surprise romantic evening for him and Bree. Cody did a lot of work and the shed looked amazing!"

"You have got to be kidding me! Cody finally got the stomach to do something. Good on him! I will have to catch up with them both soon," Thomas said warmly.

"They're busy mustering and dipping and worming the cattle today," said Beth.

"Do they need a hand?" enquired Thomas. Beth re-marked that she didn't know, but it was a big job for the two of them, even with some help from Paul. Thomas said he would be over later to help, and they both said their goodbyes.

* * *

Bree and Cody were now busy mustering the cattle on horseback; Cody went across the creek to get any cattle on that side, and then mustered them up to the yards. Bree was mustering the paddocks close to the yards and was on her way towards the cattle yards when she saw Paul's farm buggy up there. Bree was thankful that her dad had come down to help, it was going to be a big job.

'Back to work — this is not going to get done by itself, and it

has to be done soon with the warmer weather around the corner,' Bree thought.

At the cattle yards Bree called out, "Hi, Dad, I have most of the cattle, the rest are over the creek and Cody is bringing them in."

"They are looking in good condition. Looks like we might have to sell some, you don't want to overstock the paddocks. Only if you want, though," said Paul.

"Dad, is the market price alright? I was thinking the same thing, there are some calves and young ones there. We don't want too many bulls, so instead of making them steers, why don't we sell them?" suggested Bree.

"Me, well I would sell them, as we have hotter weather coming and the farm shouldn't be overstocked in the heat," Paul reasoned. "But it's all up to you."

Bree thought for a moment, and then said, "Okay, let's dip and ear tag them, and then separate them."

Bree saw Cody on his way back with a herd of cattle. Bree thought, *'Now I know why I adore him; he looks so handsome on the horse – that's my man!'*

As the day wore on Bree and Cody got to work dipping and ear tagging the cattle, and separating the ones to go to the sales. Thomas joined them and was a great help, and with Paul sitting on a drum marking off the ear tag numbers it made the job even easier.

In the afternoon Paul said he was going back to the

house as he was tired. "Thank you for your help, Dad," said Bree. "Can you ring up the trucking company and organise a truck to take the calves and younger ones to sale please?"

Thomas overheard Bree, "Bree, you don't need to wear that cost. I will ring one of the boys to bring our truck over to take your stock to the saleyards. You have all the paperwork ready, don't you?"

"Thank you, Thomas, I have all the paperwork back at the house. I was going to muster this lot up to the yards near the shed, it will be easier for the truck to get in there anyway," said Bree.

"Dad, you know where the paperwork is, don't you? Can you fill it out for me, or get mum to fill it out? You have all the tag numbers you need," Bree asked Paul.

With that, Thomas and Paul left, and Bree and Cody started to muster the rest of the cattle across to a new paddock.

"You ready there, Cody?" checked Bree.

"Yep, let them through," he answered.

They skilfully mustered the cattle to the new paddock, and on the way back Cody turned to Bree and said, "You know, there is something we haven't done for quite a while."

"What's that?

"Lying in the back of the ute and watching the sun set," said Cody.

"You're right, Cody, it's something we haven't done for a while, and I miss you cuddling me while we watch the sun go down and see the beautiful colours across the sky."

"Well, why don't we do it tonight if you feel up to it?" Cody asked.

Bree said she was tired, that it had been a long day, and by the time they got back to the house the sun would be nearly down so she suggested the next night.

"It's a date!" Cody said laughing, and with that Bree rode up to him and gave him a kiss.

CHAPTER FIFTEEN

Bree had all the paperwork completed when the truck arrived the next morning to take the calves and young ones to the stock sale. After the truck left she got back to the task of cleaning up the shed. It was now the end of September and Paul's and Beth's wedding anniversary was a month away, so it had to be cleaned up, and she had to decide where to have everything. Plus, she would have to send out invitations, so she had a bit on her hands, but she also knew Cody was beside her to help her.

Cody entered the shed and asked what Bree was up to.

"We must finish cleaning up the shed, as it's Mum's and Dad's anniversary next month and I want to hold the party here," she answered.

Cody suggested that the local hall might be better. Bree thought for a moment, and then replied, "Yes, it could be better, and all the services we'll need are already there. Well, the shed *still* needs to be cleaned up, so we better get moving on that anyway."

Paul yelled out from the front of the shed, "Bree, you there?"

"Yes, Dad, what can I do for you?"

"Thomas just rang and we got top price for the stock we sold!" said Paul excitedly.

Bree thought, '*Great, the extra money will help with my plans for the anniversary party.*'

After hours of cleaning up, rearranging, and sorting out items, they finally had the shed clean.

"Boy, we've done a good job cleaning the shed up!" said Bree.

Cody and Bree walked hand-in-hand back to the house for afternoon tea. When they arrived Paul asked them, "Have you seen the weather report? They're forecasting a week of hot weather with storms. Last thing we need is a lightning strike to start a fire, so I was wondering about our firebreaks and if they need clearing. I was going to ask you, Cody, to bring over your dad's bulldozer to clean them up. What do you think, Bree?"

Before Bree could answer Beth interrupted, "Will you both be here for dinner?"

"No Mum, I'm taking Bree out for a picnic and to watch the sunset tonight. I was going to ask if I could get some food to take for the picnic," said Cody.

"Cody, you romantic! I wish someone else was romantic," Beth said, looking in Paul's direction.

Cody gave Beth a hug, and then Beth said, "Thank you, love. I'll put together some food for you."

Getting back to Paul's comment about the firebreaks, Bree answered, "I think that would be a great idea, Dad. Cody, can you bring over your big dozer and clear our firebreaks?"

"No worries," Cody replied, "I'll be happy to organise it with Dad."

Cody couldn't wait for that night. Later that afternoon he went up to the shed and set up Bree's ute with the mattress and everything they would need to enjoy their picnic, watch the sunset, and even watch the stars twinkle in the night sky. Bree only trusted Cody to drive her ute—no one else!

Bree had a shower and decided that it was warm enough to wear jeans and a top instead of a shirt. She was looking forward to spending alone-time with Cody, and watching the sunset.

Meanwhile, Beth was in the kitchen, "Cody love, here is the picnic basket with food and drinks for you to-night," she said as she handed it to Cody.

"Thanks, Mum. What would we do without you?"

Bree and Cody left for the special spot they had found ages ago. She was looking forward to watching the sunset and taking in the brilliant colours of the sky. The sunsets were becoming more colourful now the months were warmer.

Cody parked the ute so they could lie down in the tray, and they got out and set everything up. Before getting into the tray, Bree stood and looked at the sun setting and the dramatic colours of the sky. The orange and the pink were so beautiful!

Cody had set everything up and took the food out of the picnic basket for them to eat. Beth did great work with the food and drink: roast pork, and salad with dressing, and for dessert Beth had put in slices of her famous orange cheesecake. A bottle of water and a bottle of wine also.

After eating and talking they lay back and looked up at the sky. The evening star was bright, and the sky was darkening, now filled with twinkling stars.

Bree was thinking about Cody's suggestion to have Mum and Dad's surprise anniversary party in the local hall. She finally decided, yes, it would definitely be better there.

The next day she went into town and booked the hall and spoke to the CWA ladies, and they said they would help her. They added, "Don't worry about food or setting up or anything — you just get your mum and dad here." Bree thanked them and left to go home.

Back at home Bree was busy in her bedroom. After hours of writing, and searching for addresses and phone numbers, she had invited over one hundred of her parents' friends to the anniversary party.

Then Bree went back into town to the post office while

she was running other errands. While she was in town she ordered her present for her mum and dad: a silver platter and mug, both engraved to mark the occasion. Once she had completed all of this, she thought, *'Okay, back to work, the farm is not going to run itself.'*

As Bree was heading home she noticed out to the west some clouds which she didn't like the look of. It was now early October, and fierce clouds at this time of year meant a storm was likely. She didn't like the colour of them: green-looking clouds always meant hail.

She rang Cody straight away. "Hi, look out to the west," she said quickly.

"Oh hell, that looks like a monster! I just checked the weather forecast on my phone and it did have a storm warning out for rain, destructive winds, and hail. How far are you from home?" Cody asked, concerned.

"Cody, please go to the shed and lock everything up, I'm not far away. I'll start around the house. Ring your dad. See you soon," Bree answered.

When Bree arrived home she parked BB, her ute, in the garage and she yelled for her mum. "Mum, lock down! Look!" she called out pointing at the oncoming storm-front. "Grab some firewood," she told Beth.

Bree went around to the western side of the house and started putting up the storm boards over the louvres.

The back of the house had already been cleared of things that could become projectiles in a howling wind so Bree didn't have anything to pick up there, but she grabbed an armful of firewood too and headed inside. Paul was closing all the windows and louvres up inside on the western side of the house.

Cody parked his ute alongside the garage and put the old mattress over the windscreen and tied it down. Then he ran into the house and helped them to shut everything up.

Bree snapped into control mode. "Mum, have you got the candles and lantern out on the kitchen table yet? Also, fill up some bottles of water, please!" Bree barked like a sergeant major.

"Cody, can you put ice in the Eskies, please?" Bree asked. This storm was not the first any of them had been through, but she felt this was not going to be a good one. Bree checked the weather app on her phone and it confirmed that this storm was going to be destructive. She hoped the cattle and horses would be safe, but for now she was worried for her family.

A cold wind started blowing fiercely from the west, bending the big trees out the front. The rain had started, and the sound of it on the tin roof was loud, but when the hail started, oh boy, it was deafening! It was so loud that Beth even put tissues in her ears!

The electricity supply flashed on and off. Bree knew that the wind could blow over electricity poles, so it could be back to basics for a while. The storm raged on, and Bree was looking out of the kitchen window when she saw a piece of tin roofing go flying.

"Oh hell, where did that come from?" she asked loudly over all the racket.

Cody asked Bree what was wrong, and when she told him what had just happened, he said, "You should keep away from the window." So they went to investigate inside the house to see if there was any water coming in.

Bree noticed there was water near the back door in the laundry, so they covered the washing machine and moved things up off the floor.

Thankfully the storm had nearly passed over, but now they both knew there would be damage from it. After half an hour they all went outside to check the property. Yes, a sheet of tin had definitely come off the roof over the laundry.

Cody rang his dad to see if he was okay and to see if they could borrow a tarp to cover the laundry roof. It turned out Aurora Station had missed the storm and, yes, Thomas had a big tarp, and he and a few farm workers would bring it over shortly.

The back yard was a mess from the leaves and branches strewn around by the storm. Fortunately, the water tanks and pump had no damage, but Bree would have to source a generator to run the electric pump until power was restored. Unfortunately the storm boards on the western side of the house were full of holes. *'Oh well,'* thought Bree, *'firewood!'*

Next, Bree looked to the shed and unbelievably it was still standing. Bree laughed to herself; the new shed was sure built soundly.

The front yard was a mess too: branches, leaves, and the piece of roofing tin all bent up. *'Looks like we have some work here,'* thought Bree, but her first priority was the farm.

Bree's and Cody's utes were undamaged, so after talking to Beth and Paul, they checked the farm. They headed out towards the old cattle yards first. Before they got there they could see trees blown down and fences down too.

Bree continued on to the creek. She gasped! It had been many years since she had seen the creek flowing. This time it was flooded and flowing fast, but she knew that give it two or three days, and it would be back to normal. As sunset was approaching Bree thought it best to head back home.

Thomas and his workers had arrived by now, and they had already put a yellow tarp on the roof, and were cleaning up some of the mess.

"Hi, Thomas, thanks for the tarp. It's been a long time since we've had no power, and I suppose it will be at least a week before we get the power back on here," Bree supposed.

"No, it won't. I've brought over a generator and some camping fridges. So you all should be okay for tonight anyway," Thomas told her, smiling.

"Tomorrow, I'm going to bring over a truck and a tractor and a few blokes, and we will check over the farm. You look after mum and dad and sort out the house," Thomas said, and gave Bree a hug.

Thankfully they had the combustion stove so they could cook, and they could boil water for a bath, and — most importantly — boil water for coffee.

'That is what I could go for right now!' thought Bree.

* * *

Over the following week Cody, and Thomas and his workers, cut trees down which had fallen over fences, and then mended many of the damaged fences too. The only good thing to come out of the storm was that the grass was growing, and it was green. Bree thought happily, *'At least I won't have to worry about feed for the cattle for a while.'*

Around the house, Bree and Beth got to cleaning up the front and back yards. Trees had to be trimmed, and the yards mowed. Paul tried to do some mowing, but even though it was a ride-on mower, it took it out of him, so Bree finished the job for her dad.

Everyone had a very busy week cleaning up after the storm. Bree was still amazed that the shed had got away without any damage. As usual, Cody had been extremely helpful throughout the whole event. He kept everyone calm, he showed he cared for everyone, and he had worked hard around the farm afterwards to fix everything that needed it.

It was just another way that Cody showed Bree how much he cared for her, and she knew the truth of it deep down inside her heart.

CHAPTER SIXTEEN

Another week rolled around. *'Monday morning already? Oh, boy that week went by quickly,'* thought Bree as she headed into town to work at the produce store. This was the beginning of Bree's second week back at work; however, she was on light duties only as her broken hand was not quite fully healed. She hadn't seen Cody all weekend, so she supposed he must have been helping his dad. Work came first though, so she got straight into work mode: the orders, the stock, the farmers who came in and talked.

Olivia popped in at lunch time to see Bree. "Hi, how are you going?" she asked.

Bree said she was okay, but the look on Olivia's face told her something was not right, so they headed outside to the table and chairs to talk.

Olivia said, "I know you and Cody have been getting on well, but I care about you."

"Olivia, what's the matter?" queried Bree.

"Have you seen Cody at all over the weekend?"

"Olivia, just spit it out, please! What is going on here?" demanded Bree.

"Ashley—Cody's ex—is back in town, and she was seen with Cody in town and in Huntsville over the weekend. I'm sorry, I don't mean to gossip or upset you, but when did you see or talk to him last?" questioned Olivia, while she held Bree's hands.

Olivia saw the colour drain from Bree's face. Olivia got up and went inside the produce store to get Bree a drink, and also spoke to Phil.

They both came outside to Bree who was crying by now. Olivia hugged her, and Phil said to Olivia, "Take her home." Then he turned to Bree and gently said, "Take some time off, I know this would be a shock. Remember, we love you Bree," said Phil.

They got into Olivia's car and she drove Bree home. Beth met them at the door, and when she saw the state Bree was in she was shocked. Beth and Olivia helped Bree into her bed, and then Olivia told Beth everything about Cody being seen with Ashley.

Beth couldn't believe it, she never thought Cody would do something like this. She rang Thomas to talk to him about it.

Thomas said he thought Cody was at The Flats, and Beth asked if it would be alright for Olivia to pick him up so that the two of them could drive to Bree's work and then Thomas would drive her ute home. Thomas said no worries, and he would see Beth in a while.

"You need anything else, Beth, you ring me. I don't know what that son of mine is thinking!" said Thomas.

Bree woke up after about two hours sleep. She was feeling washed out, and hurt. And she couldn't believe Ashley was back, and that Cody was spending time with her. She questioned, why did she kiss him, why did she tell him she had feelings for him? He told her he would never hurt her.

'Well, he's not allowed on this farm, I want nothing to do with him!' thought Bree. She got up and went out to the kitchen for a coffee, and Beth and Thomas were there.

Thomas walked over to her and gave her a cuddle, and asked what he could do for her. Bree started to cry, and Thomas led her to a chair while Beth made her a coffee. Bree spoke to Thomas and Beth for a while, questioning Cody's feelings for her. She told them everything that Olivia had told her, and Thomas was not happy.

"Don't worry about help, I'll organise that, and believe you me when I see Cody … well he has a lot to answer for. I will let him know not to contact you or come over here. Your ute is home—I know you are protective of it—but I drove it here and it's fine. If you want anything, or mum and dad want anything, you ring me, okay?" said Thomas.

With that, Thomas left. One of his farmhands had come to pick him up to drive him back home to Aurora Station. Hearing voices in the kitchen, Paul came into the room and Beth took him out to the verandah and told him what had happened, then she went back inside to be with her daughter. Paul was angry, but he knew he had to let Bree do what she had to.

Bree said, "Mum, I am done with Cody. Why hurt me like this? I thought I knew him." Bree's phone rang and Beth answered it; it was Cody wanting to speak with Bree.

"Cody, don't call Bree anymore, I think you had better stay away. Talk to your father. You have hurt her, and she doesn't want to talk to you," said Beth and she ended the call. Bree went back to her bedroom and started crying again, and after a while she fell asleep.

While Bree was sleeping, Beth took phone calls from Olivia, Nick, Phil, Johnno, and others wanting to know how Bree was. Many of them said they weren't talking to Cody, and they were disgusted by his actions.

Nick rang Beth the next morning and asked if he and Olivia could come out to see Bree, and Beth said "Yes, that would be fine." They picked up some food from the grocery store on their way for Beth and Paul.

"Hi, you two! Oh, what's this?" asked Beth when Nick and Olivia arrived.

Nick answered, "The groceries are for you from the store. The whole town is worried about Bree, and they're upset by what Cody has done. Thomas is really disappointed with Cody, apparently he told Ashley to never come back to Chilly when they split up last year. I just don't understand why Cody has done this."

Olivia added that Cody was calling everyone, trying to talk to Bree, but no one was talking to him. "How is she, Beth?" They sat and spoke for a while and then Bree came into the kitchen. Both Olivia and Nick got up and gave her a cuddle. Bree asked why they were there, so they told her about everyone's reaction to what Cody had done, and how they would help her.

* * *

Two weeks later — it was now mid-October — Paul and Beth had to go to Braham to see Paul's cardiologist, and Bree drove them in Paul's car. The heart specialist was not happy with Paul's progress, and he decided to put Paul on new medication. Paul complained he was like a baby rattle with all the tablets he was taking. The specialist organised help around the house for Paul and Beth as both of them were getting on in age, and Beth didn't like driving anymore.

Beth was happy with the outcome of the appointment with the specialist. Her only hope was that Paul would settle down a bit. Since Cody had upset Bree, Paul's temper had been up. Thankfully, the assistance Thomas gave them on the farm was a big help.

Even so, Beth was worried as she knew there was something wrong with Bree. Bree hadn't gone back to work in town, she had hardly left the farm, and she rarely spoke to Nick or Oliva. Beth decided she would phone Olivia and ask her what she thought might be wrong with Bree.

Around this time Bree had to go to Braham, she didn't tell Beth about *why* she had to go, just that she *had* to go. The truth was that Bree had an appointment with a psychologist. The trauma from seeing Bob again, her father's over-protectiveness, and her belief that Cody and Ashley were back together again was all too much to take. Bree felt she had not been coping and she needed help. After the consultation she felt a little better, but she knew she would need to check in regularly with the psychologist for the time being.

Bree stopped at the last fuel station between Braham and Chilly for fuel and something to eat. She knew that the road ahead needed her full concentration because it had many sharp corners. Bree finished her drink and her snack, and then set off home. She rang Beth and let her know she was leaving the fuel station, and said she would see her in about an hour or so. It was going to be dark before she arrived home.

Bree drove cautiously as she listened to the radio, singing along to her favourite songs, when one came on that she and Cody had slow-danced to at the rodeo ball. She started crying uncontrollably, and with her vision blurred she could not see the road clearly. At the worst possible moment a kangaroo hopped in front of her; Bree swerved hard to avoid it and lost control of the ute which was now skidding from side to side. She never saw the tree her ute slammed into.

* * *

Time passed, Bree was late getting home, and she wasn't answering her phone. Beth was worried; she knew something must have happened, so she phoned Thomas.

"Thomas, can you help me, please?" Beth asked, with panic in her voice.

Thomas said, "What's wrong, Beth? You don't sound well." Beth told him that Bree had gone to Braham and had not returned, and that she wasn't answering her phone. "I will be over in a minute."

When Thomas arrived at the farm Beth came out of the house to meet him. "You got the coffee on, Beth?" he asked.

"Yes, always. Please come in, Thomas," said Beth.

"Okay, do you have a map showing the road to Braham?" Beth pulled out the map and spread it on the kitchen table.

"Thanks. So Bree is not answering her phone at all? Have you tried the UHF?" enquired Thomas.

"UHF no, and her phone rings out," said Beth.

Paul was hopping mad, angry that Bree wasn't picking up her phone, but also panic-stricken that his little girl might be in trouble. He wasn't thinking clearly and he wasn't talking sense. In fact, he was getting in the way, so Beth told Paul to be quiet as he was not helping the situation. Beth and Thomas were doing their best to ignore him and keep their conversation on track.

"Okay, can you ring Bree's friends and ask them to head to Braham, and to keep an eye out for Bree's ute. If they see anything they are to ring you or me," instructed Thomas.

Thomas rang the Chilly police station and told them about Bree. They contacted Braham police who said they would start their search from the Braham end, heading back towards Chilly. Thomas, all of Bree's friends, and even Johnno from the pub, headed to Braham.

Thomas was driving when Cody rang him. "Cody, I don't have time to talk to you now, Bree has gone missing. She was on her way back from Braham, but she hasn't made it home." Thomas said quickly.

"I don't understand why nobody rang me to tell me about this?" Cody asked his father, confused.

Thomas pulled his car over to the side of the road, so he could concentrate on the call. "You have hurt Bree deeply by getting back with that Ashley. Why do you think no one will talk to you, or have anything to do with you? Ashley, really? After what she did to you over a year ago. Boy, you need to wake up! I have to go and find Bree." And with that, Thomas ended the call to Cody.

Cody was in Chilly at the pub, and after his father hung up on him, he went up to the bar for another lite beer. Jenny was serving at the bar and she asked Cody if he was alright.

"No, Bree has gone missing, and I have just found out Ashley has caused problems—yet again."

Jenny said, "That Ashley has been in the pub saying she was getting married to you, and that you didn't feel anything for Bree, and that Bree was just a fill-in."

"What did you say? No way would I marry that witch!" exclaimed Cody. Jenny told him to settle down and they talked about what Ashley had said, and Jenny told Cody that Ashley had told her story to everyone in town.

Hearing the lies that Ashley had put around made Cody so mad. He drove to the motel where Ashley was staying without thinking about his speed. When he arrived he pulled up so quickly the tyres on his ute squealed. Ashley came out from her motel room with her arms open to greet Cody.

"How dare you!" Cody yelled at Ashley. "What do you think you are up to? I would never marry you in a blue fit, you mean nothing to me. You've spread rumours about me so that even my own father won't talk to me. I want you out of town in an hour! Never come anywhere near me or my family, or Bree and her family ever again. I'll be ringing my solicitor and taking action against you for the rumours and damage you have caused. Never contact me again, hear me— never!" Cody got back into his ute and headed towards The Flats.

When Cody pulled up at The Flats Beth came outside.

Cody said to her, "Please don't say a thing. Ashley has done so much damage. I was *never, ever* getting back with her or marrying that witch of a woman. Please, Beth, is there any news about Bree? That's all I am worried about."

Beth said, "Slow down, Cody, come inside and get a coffee. I guessed it was something to do with Ashley. Yes, Bree is hurting about you and Ashley, but first we must find her."

They went inside and Beth made coffee for Cody. She told him about Bree's movements, and he started to cry, and Beth cuddled him. All Cody kept saying was, "I love her … where is she?"

After a hot coffee and a good talk, it was decided that Cody would head towards Braham to see if he could find Bree. On the way he rang Nick and Rick, and explained that Ashley had lied, and that there was nothing going on between them. They understood him, and agreed that if they found Bree they would let Cody know.

After nearly two hours of driving, Cody was getting really worried. Suddenly, he saw something out of the corner of his eye. He turned his ute around to get a better look, and as he did the headlights shone on the back of Bree's ute, partially hidden by trees by the side of the road.

"No! No! No!" was all Cody could say as he ran to Bree's ute. He opened the driver's door to see her slumped forward, she was lifeless, and she had a nasty cut to her head. Cody immediately rang triple-zero.

CHAPTER SEVENTEEN

The triple-zero operator answered.

"Hi, my name is Cody Patrick, I've just found Bree Douglas who has been missing. She's had a car accident, looks like she ran off the road and hit a tree. I need ambulance and police, to Main Road … on the Braham side, just before you get to the Dutchman's Road turnoff."

The triple-zero operator asked a series of questions: Is she breathing? Does she have a pulse? Is she bleeding anywhere? And so on. Cody replied that Bree was breathing, but unconscious, she had a cut to her head and the airbags of the ute had gone off.

The operator asked if Cody could access the battery of the ute. Cody answered that he had already disconnected it. Soon Cody could hear sirens approaching, so the triple-zero operator ended the call. A police four-wheel drive, followed by an ambulance arrived in what seemed like only seconds.

The paramedics checked Bree's vital signs first. The

police officer moved Cody away from Bree's ute and took all the details from him. Cody wanted to go to Bree, but the police officer wouldn't let him. Instead, he asked Cody to wait near his own ute. While standing at his ute watching the paramedics working on Bree he rang his dad.

"Dad," Cody said, and he started crying.

"Cody, what's wrong? Talk to me," said Thomas as he pulled his car off the road.

"I've found Bree near Dutchman's Road. Her ute has come off the road and has hit a tree," replied Cody. "She's hurt and the paramedics are taking her to Braham General Hospital. I won't leave her. Please tell Paul and Beth, and let them know I'll stay with Bree until they arrive."

Thomas said "Okay, son, I'll organise a motel room for us in Braham. I'll arrange to have Bree's ute towed once the police are finished with it. Take Bree's handbag out of the ute … and drive safely."

"Dad, can you ring Rick and tell him what's happened, and get him to pass on the word?" Cody said through his tears.

"No worries. I will see you when we get to the hospital," said Thomas.

At the hospital, Cody waited to hear any news about Bree. After some time a doctor came out to the waiting area to see him. He explained that Bree was still unconscious, due to her head injury. Even though the airbags had inflated, it was thought she must have hit her head hard on the side pillar because it looked like the ute had skidded from side to side.

The doctor was also concerned that Bree may have some amnesia, so she may not remember how, or what, happened for her to run off the road and hit the tree. Bree needed an x-ray of her spine and pelvis to make sure she had no injuries there. She also had bruising to her stomach from the seatbelt. The doctor said it could take some time for Bree to regain consciousness. Cody asked to see Bree, but the doctor said Cody could go to her after she was transferred to a bed in the intensive care unit (ICU).

A while later Thomas, Beth, and Paul arrived. Cody filled them in on what he knew about the accident and Bree's current condition. He started to cry, and Paul went to him. "Son, come on, Bree is in the best place now, don't worry about the ute or anything else. You pull yourself together," said Paul.

"Dad, Bree and I have not been talking because Ashley is in town, and she put around we were getting married. No way! I love Bree so much. I hate that she is hurt, and I'm so worried about her," said Cody.

Thomas said, "Son, let's forget about that now, and concentrate on Bree. I will talk to her when she is conscious." He faced Beth and asked, "Beth, why was Bree in Braham?" Beth replied that she didn't know.

Later Bree was moved to a bed in the intensive care unit, and Beth and Paul spoke to the doctor who was looking after her. Beth was allowed in to sit beside Bree's bed.

Beth said in a quiet voice, "Bree, my girl, you need to wake up. You have a bloke here who is in tears and is worried about you. You are as stubborn as your dad sometimes. Cody is *not* marrying Ashley. He loves you, and he found you, sweetheart. Please wake up."

It was teatime so Thomas, Paul, and Cody went to check into the motel and get something to eat. Cody didn't want anything to eat; he just wanted Bree to wake up so he could tell her he loved her.

The doctor said it would be best if Beth went and got some rest, and if Bree woke up he would ring her. However, the doctor didn't think Bree would wake up anytime soon considering the hit to her head.

Back at the motel they all sat around and spoke, and Cody gave Bree's handbag to Beth. Thomas told Beth and Paul that the police had released Bree's ute, and he had already had it towed back to Chilly where Rick had inspected it. Thomas had spoken to Rick, who had found the brakes worked fine — just a bit of wear — and all the tyres were still inflated.

The next morning Beth received a phone call to say that Bree was waking up. They all headed to the hospital, and Beth and Paul went straight in to see Bree. Beth told Bree that Cody found her, and that he was upset and worried about her, and that he couldn't stop crying. Bree said she didn't want to talk to him. Beth held Bree's hand and gently began explaining everything that had happened.

Paul came out to the waiting area and spoke to Thomas and Cody. "Sorry, son, but Bree doesn't want to see you. One word: Ashley." This upset Cody, and he fell into a chair and started to cry. Paul sat next to him and said, "Give her time, she has not long woken up and Beth is talking to her." Then Paul added, "Thomas, why don't you go in and see Bree?"

Turning back to Cody, Paul said, "Cody, son, I care about you, and I can see you are hurting. I know Bree means the world to you, and it's about time you did something about it."

Cody said, "Dad, I haven't rushed Bree into a physical relationship after what happened to her with Bob, and it's killing me. I've told Bree I love her, and I know she has strong feelings for me, but she hasn't said *those* three words, and she said she isn't ready for anything more yet. I'm letting her call the shots."

Paul said, "Time for you to make a move. It can go either way. It's your choice."

Cody walked out of the hospital, he needed time to think and work out how he could talk to Bree. He checked his phone, there were missed calls and text messages. He sat on a bench under a big shady tree and answered the text messages.

Thomas came outside and found him, "Cody, son, are you okay?"

"Dad, I love Bree so much, and it hurts that she doesn't want to talk to me. That rotten woman Ashley has done so much damage! How do I get Bree back?"

"Son, she's just woken up, and she has had a terrible accident. Beth has spoken to her and explained everything. Nothing else can be done other than to wait," Thomas replied.

Later, back inside the hospital, the doctor spoke to all of them, and he told them that Bree was being moved to a ward, and he felt she was improving daily. The doctor said she could go home tomorrow if the x-rays were clear.

Beth took Thomas aside and spoke to him quietly, "Thomas, how can we repay you for everything you have done for us?" enquired Beth.

"Beth, you owe me nothing. I'm glad Bree is alright, and you know she is like a daughter to me. I spoke to Cody—oh, and Paul spoke to him as well. He's not handling everything too well. He loves Bree so much and he's frightened of losing her because of the damage that Ashley woman has done," Thomas said.

Beth touched Thomas's arm, "Let's sit down. I spoke to Bree, as you know, and I told her everything. She is just like Paul, stubborn, but I got through to her. She doesn't want to see Cody at the moment, and I think it best we deal with them at home. I suggest we send

Cody home to our farm to work, and hopefully that will settle him down a bit." Thomas nodded his agreement to Beth's suggestion.

After Thomas and Beth spoke to Cody he headed home to The Flats, all the time he was driving he was thinking about Bree. When he got to the farm he spoke to the farmhands Thomas had looking after the farm. Farm work was just what Cody needed!

After another day Bree was released from hospital with orders: no working, no farm work. She had to rest up for a couple of weeks. Thomas drove them all back to The Flats. He had rung ahead to Cody, who got help to clean up the house, and brought food and firewood in. The house was so clean and tidy that it looked like a display home. The only rooms not touched were Bree's bedroom, and Beth's and Paul's bedroom.

The house was like a florist's shop because so many people had sent flowers for Bree. Cody arranged them all through the lounge room. Cody had wanted to put some flowers in Bree's bedroom, but he respected her so much that he did not go into her room, he actually shut the door on it. Cody had organised one of the CWA ladies to cook some meals and some cakes, and she arrived with them all. Beth's fridge was full! Cody thought that was one thing that Beth did not have to worry about when she came home, she could just take care of Bree.

Cody moved his things up to the little bedroom in the

shed. As much as he wanted to stay in the house and be close to Bree, he thought it best to go to the shed and give her some space.

Back at the house, Cody heard a car pull up and he went outside—they had arrived home. Paul greeted Cody, and Cody told him how the house was clean, that there was plenty of food, and that he had moved to the shed. Paul shook his head side to side. Cody asked how Bree was. Paul said she was on the mend, but the drive home had made her tired. Cody said he had work to do, and he would see them at lunch time.

Cody walked past Beth and Bree, he touched his hat and said, "Hi." Paul spoke with Thomas and shared what Cody had been doing, and Thomas then went in search of Cody.

Back in the house, Beth and Bree were amazed at how clean it was, and how many flowers there were. All the flowers still had their cards on them, and Beth said, "Bree, you will have to send a thank you card to them all." Bree said she was tired, and that she was going to go and lie down.

When she went into her bedroom she looked out the window towards the shed and she could see Thomas hugging Cody. Bree's heart skipped a beat on seeing Cody again. She knew she had misjudged him, but she was scared; she did not want to get hurt again.

Bree went back out to the kitchen. "Mum, what happened to my ute?"

Beth said, "Don't worry about it, Thomas had it towed to Rick's shop. He knew you would not want it anywhere else. I'm sorry, but the insurance company has written it off. The airbags went off and the damage was bad. When you are better you can get a new one."

"Mum, can we talk please?" Beth was worried, she had never seen Bree like this before. "Mum, I was too hard on Cody, but hearing about him and Ashley … well, I thought he had left me. You know the damage Bob did to me … Mum, I want to move on, but I'm frightened, even though I know Cody loves me."

Beth held Bree's hand and said, "Bree, you cannot live in the past. You may not fully see it, but you can trust Cody. Yes, that woman has made a fool of him, and I know he feels awful about being so blind to her actions. Cody has moved all his things up to the shed and he is going to sleep up there. He thinks you wouldn't want him around you. You know, he is hurting too, sweetheart."

Beth took a breath and continued, "When Cody found out you were missing he was beside himself, it took both Thomas and your Dad to settle him down. Cody said he was going to find you if it meant walking the road to and from Braham! Cody found you, Bree. You need to stop looking back at the past. Your future is so bright, if you would only look forward." Bree cuddled her mum tightly.

Bree rang Olivia, "Hi, Olivia, I'm home now, and I

wonder if you could come out to the farm, please. I'll fill you in when you get here."

"No worries Bree, see you soon."

About half an hour later Olivia pulled up at The Flats. She went to the back door where Bree met her, and they hugged gently, mindful of Bree's injuries. "I'm so glad to see you up and about. I suppose you haven't seen your ute. Bree, it's really bad. Rick's looking after it, but he said it's a write-off."

"Yes, Mum told me the insurance company has written it off. I will catch up with everyone soon. The reason I asked you out here is that I need your help," explained Bree. "Prior to my accident I had started work on Mum's and Dad's surprise wedding anniversary party. I've booked the local hall and sent out the invitations, and I have all the RSVPs. But I can't do anything at the moment, and I was wondering if you could take over the planning for me."

Olivia responded, "Of course I will help you out. When is the party?"

"I have booked the hall in town for next Saturday — sorry, I know it's short notice, but the CWA ladies are helping with some of it," said Bree.

They talked for almost an hour about everything else that needed to be done for Beth's and Paul's surprise anniversary party, and then Olivia left. Bree was happy now, she knew the party would go ahead, and she really wanted that for her Mum and her Dad.

CHAPTER EIGHTEEN

Bree decided it was time she talked to Cody.

"Dad, do you know where Cody is? " she asked Paul.

"Cody is up at the shed," replied Paul. "Are you okay, girly?"

"I'm fine, Dad. Could I ask you to go and ask Cody to come down here? I want to talk to him."

"No worries, Bree, I will go and get Cody."

Cody was busy working in the shed when he heard Paul arrive on his buggy.

"Cody, my boy, could you please clean yourself up? Bree asked me to come up and get you, she wants to talk to you about something," said Paul.

"No worries. Everything okay, Paul?" asked Cody. "Son, Bree just asked me to come up and get you. Better drive your ute down."

Cody cleaned up and put on a fresh shirt, and then headed down to the house.

'*What does Bree want to talk to me about?*' Cody wondered.

Bree was waiting outside for Cody when he reached the house.

"Hi, Cody. Firstly, thank you for everything you have done for me, from finding me in the ute to all the work you have done here on the farm. Secondly, I was wondering if you could take me for a drive later this afternoon, out to the tree line? I would like to talk to you about something," said Bree.

"No worries, I can do that," replied Cody.

"Okay, then. I'll ask Mum to put together a nice picnic dinner for us."

Later that afternoon, Cody arrived at the house to pick Bree up. He was concerned how she would go getting into his ute after her accident. He helped her from the house, and when they got to his ute, he stopped and asked her if she would be alright to get into it.

Bree said, "Thank you, I think I will be alright." Cody helped Bree into the ute, and then got in himself.

Cody drove slowly, and tried to make the trip as smooth as possible, so that Bree was not bouncing around in her seat.

When they got to the tree line, Cody asked Bree if she wanted to get out and sit on the tray. He had put the old mattress in the back for her to sit on.

"I don't think I could get up there by myself, but could

you lift me up, please?" Bree asked.

Bree thought, '*Oh, it feels so good to be in Cody's strong arms again.*' She had missed that feeling.

Cody and Bree sat down on the mattress, and she rested against the toolbox. Cody had the picnic basket that Beth had made for them, out on the tray too.

"Cody, what I want to talk to you about is us," said Bree. "When I heard you were with Ashley, and you would not answer my phone calls, I thought you had left me. It hurt, and I remembered you said you would never hurt me. I didn't know that Ashley fooled you and used you. It wasn't until I spoke to Mum, Dad, and Thomas, that I understood what really went on." Cody said nothing, so Bree continued, "I told you, a while back now, how strong my feelings were for you. I *still* have those feelings, Cody. I care about you more than you can ever know. I'm sorry I misjudged your feelings for me. Can you ever forgive me?"

Cody looked at Bree, he did not say a word. He moved closer to her, and he cupped her face in his big hands and kissed Bree passionately on the lips. Bree wrapped her arms around Cody.

Then Cody pulled back and said to Bree, "I feel that I have hurt you, with that Ashley thing. I'm angry that I couldn't protect you from the car accident, and now you're *still* hurting. I want to forget all about Ashley and her drama. I was blind. You mean the world to me, and when I found you in the ute … my heart raced so fast. I didn't want you hurt, but seeing you injured and not being able to do anything to help you — well, let's say I cried all the way into Braham following the ambulance." Cody brushed back a strand of hair from Bree's face, and added, "I know you have feelings for me but, Brenda Douglas, I *love* you, have done for a long time. Please forgive me for ever hurting you."

Bree and Cody held on tightly to each other, not wanting to let go. Finally when they parted Bree said she was hungry and thirsty, and she asked Cody what Mum had packed into the picnic basket. So, while watching the sunset they had a picnic of freshly-made sandwiches and home-grown fruit.

After they had finished eating Bree looked directly at Cody and said, "I want you to move your things back into the house, the shed is not good enough for you to live in. And anyway I want to be closer to you."

Cody grinned and said, "Okay, if you insist! Thanks."

A couple of days later Bree had arranged with Cody for him to take her to Braham. She had to attend a follow-up visit with the doctor after being discharged from hospital, and she had to look at a new ute. Cody drove carefully all the way; Bree had slid over to the middle seat to sit next to Cody.

Bree was glad to reach Braham, the drive had made her hips and back ache. When they got to Braham Cody found a coffee shop and got them a take-away coffee each and they walked to the park in the centre of town. Bree walked around slowly, trying to ease the pain in her hips.

"Cody, could you please rub my back for me?" Bree asked him. "It hasn't enjoyed the drive from home to here." Cody gently rubbed her back for a little while until she said that it was better.

A while later they headed to Bree's appointment at the doctors. She was given the all-clear to do a little work in short bursts, and she was told if she needed anything else she could phone the medical practice to save the trip to Braham.

Cody and Bree then headed to the car yard. Bree looked at the utes and Cody checked them out more closely. Bree decided on a new one, just an updated model of her old ute. But—she wanted it in black. The salesman asked her to wait while he phoned the dealership in Triton to see if they had a black ute in stock. He went inside to make the call and when he came back outside he said, "You are one lucky lady! You have the last black ute in the country." Bree smiled back at him.

It would be a couple of weeks before Bree got it. He asked about spotlights, etc., but Bree said she already had all that and more.

Cody took it steadily home; he even stopped a couple of times so Bree could walk around and gently stretch her legs, hips and back. When they got back to the house Beth and Paul greeted them.

"Cody, son, I have moved all your stuff out of the shed into the spare room today. Anyway, Bree, what did the doctor say?"

Bree told her mum and dad what the doctor had said, and she also told them about the ute. Bree said she was tired, and she would see them in the morning. Cody got up and helped her to her bedroom. Cody stopped at the door, and asked, "Will you be alright from here on, Bree?"

Bree turned to Cody and wrapped her arms around him, "Cody you can come into my bedroom, it's okay. You know the one thing I have missed? Remember the camping trip where you cuddled me to sleep, and after the court case too, well I have missed that so much."

"Are you sure about me coming into your bedroom?" asked Cody.

Bree said, "Yes, I am, Cody. I know I can trust you." Bree went and changed her clothes in the bathroom, and when she returned she lay down on the bed, and Cody lay down beside her and cuddled her until she went to sleep. Once he was sure that Bree was sound asleep, Cody quietly left her room.

"Mum, any chance of a coffee, please?" Cody asked as he entered the kitchen.

Beth gave Cody an odd look. "Sit down, son, here you go. Has Bree gone off to sleep?" she asked.

Cody told Beth she had, and then he told her about the

picnic and what Bree had just said. Cody respected Paul and Beth, and he asked Beth if she was okay with him going into Bree's room.

"Cody, I am fine with everything. It looks like Bree has seen that she was wrong about everything to do with Ashley, and I had a big talk with her about everything that has happened recently, and it sounds like Bree is finally moving forward."

* * *

The next day Bree phoned Olivia; it was only two days before Beth's and Paul's surprise wedding anniversary party on the 31st of October. Bree asked Olivia, "How am I going to get Mum and Dad into town?"

Olivia suggested, "Phone Thomas to see if he could bring them into town. He could just say that he was taking them out to tea at the pub." Bree said, "Great idea! I'll ring Thomas now."

Bree ended her call with Olivia, and dialled Thomas's number straight away. "Hi Thomas, how are you?" she enquired.

"Hi Bree, I'm fine, but how are you going? Cody said you're waiting on your new ute," said Thomas. Bree spoke to him about the problem of getting Beth and Paul into town for the party. Thomas agreed to the plan Olivia suggested, and they made a time for him to be at the house.

Bree then phoned Cody and asked if he could take her

into town for the party. Cody assured her he would take her into town, but he just had to go home and get some clothes first. He then asked Bree, "Do you need anything from town?"

Bree said the only thing she needed was to pick up her present for her Mum and Dad from the jeweller, and then give it to Olivia, and Cody kindly agreed to do all of that for her.

At dinner that night Bree told Beth and Paul that she was taking them into the pub for dinner the following night as a thank-you for everything they had done. She added, "And Mum needs a break from cooking now that the weather is warming up!"

For the party Bree chose to wear a dress that was nice and cool, and she wore low heels. Cody and Thomas arrived at the house at the same time. Everyone was dressed in light, cool clothing as the weather had been hot already. They got into their cars and away they went. Thomas knew he had to go to the community hall, so Bree was not worried about that, but she knew Paul and Beth would have a million questions. Cody and Bree arrived before Thomas, Beth, and Paul.

"Where are you going?" Paul asked Thomas as he drove straight past the pub. Thomas said, "I'm under orders from Bree."

When Thomas, Paul, and Beth arrived at the hall, all Bree said to her parents was, "Quiet," and when they got to the door of the hall she said, "Close your eyes and do not open them until I say to." Thomas and Cody helped her to get them inside. Once they were all inside and the doors were closed, Bree said to Paul and Beth, "Open your eyes!"

Beth could not believe what she saw. The hall was decorated, old friends stood in front of her, and there were pictures and old photos everywhere. Beth looked down to see the guest book from their wedding open with plenty of heartfelt messages from friends and family already written in it. It was then she noticed the sign on the table. Beth touched Paul and said, "Look."

Bree came over to both of them, gave them a hug and said, "Happy wedding anniversary, Mum and Dad."

Beth asked Bree how she managed to do all of this, and Bree called Olivia over to them. "Mum, Olivia here pulled all this together, because I had my accident. If it had not been for Olivia, well, none of this would have happened."

Beth and Paul welcomed everyone, chatting to this one and that one. The party went really well. Thanks to the CWA ladies the food was amazing, and the music kept people dancing all night, but it was not too loud to be enjoyable. When it came time for gifts to be opened Beth was blown away with the gift from Bree. Bree had a wedding photo of her parents mounted into a beautiful silver picture frame, plus there was the exquisite silver platter and silver mug, all engraved especially to mark the occasion.

At the end of the night Beth and Paul thanked every-one for coming to the party, especially those who had helped to make it a success. Thomas drove Paul and Beth home, and Cody drove Bree home.

When they arrived home, Bree said to Cody, "Let's go and sit on the logs out the back." Cody took the blanket out of the car and put it over the logs. "Mum and Dad's party went well, thanks to Olivia. And thank *you* for everything you did for tonight, Cody. I'm so grateful for all your help. I will be glad for things to get back to normal, though," admitted Bree.

Cody said, "You know I would do anything for you, Bree, all you have to do is ask. The party was great for sure, and Olivia did *so* well. She needs to start a party planning business!"

Bree turned around to Cody, she looked straight into his eyes and reached her hand up to touch his face. Cody bent his head down and they kissed passionately under the stars.

CHAPTER NINETEEN

It was now early November, and the weather was really starting to heat up. Even though she was recovering, Bree was still unable to do much work on the farm, and she had not yet returned to work at the produce store, but she helped Cody as much as she could. She asked him about how he was getting on with the firebreaks and he replied that he had made a good start on them.

In mid-November Bree's new ute arrived. The dealership in Braham received her new ute earlier than expected and they shipped it straight to her farm. Cody, Beth, and Paul were there when the ute was backed off the truck. Bree signed all the paperwork, and the truck left to return to the dealership.

Bree looked over her new ute. She asked Cody, "Would you come for a run with me? I want to drive to Rick's auto shop and show him my new ute."

Cody asked if had she been cleared to drive, and she confirmed that she had been given the all-clear. As Cody and Bree drove out of the farm, he noticed she was driving a bit slower than normal, and he asked if she was alright. "Yes, it's just been a while since I drove," Bree answered.

They pulled up at Rick's shop and he came out to greet them. "Gee, Bree, it looks good … but it's missing some stuff," said Rick.

"Yes, I know it's missing some things, and you know I hate these skinny tyres. So, on the list is tyres for a start. You have all my spotlights etc., from my old ute don't you?" she asked.

Rick brought out everything he had rescued from Bree's old ute, BB. "Bree, I'm sorry, but you're going to need new spotlights as these are broken, and they can't be repaired. Also your UHF aerial is broken. Hang on … did you have insurance for them too?"

Bree said that she did, and she rang her insurance company straight away. The customer service representative she spoke to checked Bree's policy regarding additional lights and accessories, and then checked Bree's claim file. She confirmed that the insurance company had approved new spotlights, a new UHF aerial, and a new bullbar for Bree's new ute.

Bree updated Rick about this and they went into his office where she picked out all the new accessories. She asked Rick when he would be able to fit everything, and he said, "In a week or two, if that's okay."

And so, a date was set for just over two weeks' time for Rick to have Bree's new ute for two days, so that he could fit all the new accessories on to it.

***

Cody continued to work on the firebreaks and Bree checked on the cattle by driving Paul's buggy. She missed riding Hayson, but she had not been given clearance to ride him yet.

Cody came in from a full day's work, dusty and sweaty, so he headed for a shower. Beth had dinner ready when he returned from the bathroom, and after dinner Cody and Bree went for a drive.

Cody said, "You have a birthday coming up, what would you like?"

Bree answered, "Well, you know I can ask you the same question."

Then Bree said to Cody jokingly, "A new body that isn't wrecked!" They both laughed.

The next morning, Cody got up early and looked for Paul. "Morning, Paul, how are you doing today?" Cody asked.

"Hot already, son, this summer is going to be scorching. How are you going?"

Cody answered that he was going okay, and that he had nearly finished all the firebreaks. Cody looked around to see if anyone else was up. "Paul, I have something to ask you, but I need you to keep it just between us," said Cody.

"Son, what's on your mind?"

"Um … I was wondering if, … um …" Cody could not get the right words out.

"Son, for goodness sake will you stop beating around the bush and just ask me what you want to ask me!" Paul said impatiently.

"Here goes … Paul can I have your permission, well your permission and Beth's permission, to ask for Bree's hand in marriage, please?" Cody asked finally.

"Son, it has taken you *so* long to come and ask me, that I was starting to think you would never ask. Yes, you have our permission." Then Paul broke into a smile and added, "So how long will we have to wait for grandkids? If it is anything like you asking Bree to marry you I will be dead before any grandkids arrive," laughed Paul.

Cody laughed too, and then said, "That's something Bree and I haven't discussed yet."

Cody reached over and shook Paul's hand. "Please don't say anything about this to Bree, as I'm hoping to take her away to the mountains for two nights and ask her there. I'll speak to Dad about getting someone over to look after the farm for a couple of days."

"Son, don't worry I won't say anything … oh, just to Beth, of course. When are you planning to do this?"

"Bree's birthday is next weekend, so I was thinking about taking her up on Friday night and then coming back on Sunday afternoon," said Cody.

Cody worked the farm as well as making all the arrangements for the stay in the mountains. He went into town to see Olivia, and he told her of his plans. He asked Olivia not to say anything about it to Bree, and he also asked Olivia to help him pick out the perfect engagement ring.

The old jeweller in Chilly had some traditional jewellery, but Cody wanted a certain type of ring, so he and Olivia met up in Braham at a jewellers that Olivia knew well. After about an hour looking at rings, Cody made a decision. He bought an exquisite ring that had a large brilliant-cut solitaire diamond in the centre, and was surrounded by smaller brilliant-cut white diamonds in a classic cluster style, all set in white gold.

Cody would be back another time to buy the matching wedding bands and to have all the rings engraved.

* * *

Over dinner one night shortly afterwards, Bree's birthday came up in conversation. Paul had spoken to Beth, and they both knew what Cody had planned. Bree said she did not want anything for her birthday, but Beth said she would *have* to hold a birthday party for her.

"No, Mum!" was Bree's response to Beth's suggestion.

Over the next few days Bree did light work around the farm, and she caught up on some farm paperwork too. She was hoping to go back to work at the produce store the following week, just for a few hours, to see how she handled it.

Olivia came out to the farm that afternoon to see Bree and to check on how she was getting along.

"Hey, I'm going to Braham shopping tomorrow, do you want to come with me? You could do with a relaxing time at the hairdresser. Nails and hair. How does that sound?" Without waiting for Bree to respond Olivia continued, "Oh, and I have to buy a nice dress, Nick is taking me out to dinner on the weekend."

Bree said, "I don't know, Olivia, I think I'm okay for all of that."

Olivia said firmly, "No, I will pick you up early and we'll go to Braham for the day. I'll let Cody know."

The next morning Olivia arrived nice and early—the heat gets bad early out in the west—so at that time of year it was better travelling in the early morning or the early evening. Olivia and Bree left and headed to Braham, and Bree thought, *'Oh, how nice the air-conditioning is in Olivia's car, it's going to be hot in Braham.'*
Olivia and Bree arrived just as the shops were opening, and Olivia had already booked appointments for the two of them at the day spa.

After about two hours, with clean, styled hair and their nails done, Olivia and Bree stepped into Olivia's favourite dress shop.

"Bree, if you see anything you like, why don't you try

it on? It will be my treat," said Olivia.

Bree was looking through the racks when she spotted a soft pink cocktail dress, and thought, *'why not?'* When Bree came out of the fitting room in the dress, Olivia was amazed at how pretty Bree looked. The dress consisted of a fitted strapless underdress in pink satin, with a sheer pink chiffon overlay which was decorated with embroidery and beading in the same pink tone, and was also sprinkled with some rhinestones for a little sparkle. It was form-fitting to Bree's trim body—nipped in at the waist—and it had a full skirt ending above the knee.

Olivia told Bree that she looked beautiful in the dress, and didn't she have some pretty sandals she could wear with it? Bree thought Olivia was right about this, so she decided to take the dress, but only if Olivia let her pay for half. The two friends agreed about the payment, and then they headed to the hotel for lunch.

By the time they finished lunch it was 2 p.m. and Olivia said, "I know it's hot, but would it be okay if we headed home now?" Bree replied that she was happy to head home as she was feeling a bit tired.

They drove for a while, but then Bree started to feel uneasy. On the return journey to Chilly, Bree would pass by the exact spot where her accident happened just before the turnoff to Dutchman's Road. Olivia could see that Bree was struggling, so she pulled the car over to the side of the road in a shady spot, and stopped. She asked Bree if she was feeling alright.

Bree said, "This is where I had my accident—right here. I can't remember how or why the ute ran off the road, I just remember it was here."

Olivia put on some music, and they chatted for a bit, and then she continued driving them both home. Olivia kept Bree talking, and before long they were back at The Flats.

Olivia helped bring in Bree's dress from the car, and she took the opportunity to take Beth aside to tell her about Bree's reaction at Dutchman's Road, and to explain that Bree was feeling tired. Olivia and Bree then said their goodbyes, and Bree thanked Olivia for taking her shopping to Braham. Then she headed to her bedroom for a sleep.

Later that afternoon Cody handed a lite beer to Paul. Paul asked him, "Well, son, how is all the planning for the weekend away going?"

"All booked. I spoke to Dad, and he has organised a couple of his farmhands to come over for the weekend. They'll be camping at the shed. Biggest thing now is to get Bree to agree to come away with me."

That night after dinner, Cody and Bree went outside to sit in the cool of the evening. Beth had set up a table and chairs under the big, shady tree in the front yard, and they sat there.

Cody said, "I have a surprise for you for your

birthday. I'm taking you away for the weekend. I'm not telling you where now, though. Only thing is you must pack for two nights away. Also, make sure you put in something nice to wear as I have a special dinner organised. Your mum and dad know, and I have organised with my dad for a couple of blokes to come over and look after the farm."

"Thanks, Cody, but you don't have to do that."

"I know I don't *have* to do that, but I *want* to, and it's all booked and organised. So, we leave early Friday morning," said Cody.

No amount of saying 'no' was getting Bree anywhere. So in the end she agreed.

The weather forecast was for hot weather and storms. Bree worried about the possibility of storms while she was away, but Beth told her to stop worrying, that it would all be fine.

Early on Friday morning, Cody arrived at The Flats to pick up Bree. He put her suitcase in the tray of his ute and tied both his suitcase and hers down. After their goodbyes to Beth and Paul, Bree went to Cody's ute to find seat covers on the seats and the ute clean inside. Cody had spent a few hours the day before cleaning the inside of his ute. And then away they went, heading to the hills.

"How are you feeling?" asked Cody. "Let me know if you need me to pull up for you to stretch your legs."

"Are you going to tell me where we're going, Cody?" Bree asked.

"No," he said, grinning at her. "You will work it out later. Why don't you slide over here and rest against me. Even have a nap. We have, oh, about two hours of driving ahead of us."

"What! Why? Please tell me where we are going," Bree pleaded. Cody, would not say a word, he just kept on grinning. The air-conditioning in Cody's ute brought relief from the December heat, so Bree slid over next to him on the bench seat, and ended up falling asleep with her head resting on his shoulder.

All the while, Cody hoped the team at their holiday destination had done all that he had requested!

CHAPTER TWENTY

After driving for about an hour Bree woke up.

"Where are we?" she asked Cody, sleepily.

"Soon we will start to climb up into the mountains. You'll feel the weather change then, it should be nice and cool," Cody commented.

Bree still had no idea where they were going until she saw a sign for the holiday houses.

"Are we going to Mountain View Holiday Homes?" she questioned.

He answered with a grin, "Yes, you guessed right."

"Why?" asked Bree.

"After the year you had — unexpectedly coming across Bob, the run-in with Douglas Brighton Jr., and the court case following that, not to mention the storm and the car accident — I wanted to do something special for you," explained Cody. Then he added, "Plus it's your birthday next week."

"Oh, Cody, you didn't have to do this, but … thank

you. I can't wait to see the holiday homes, I've seen great reviews online about the place," said Bree.

About an hour later Cody pulled up in front of reception and asked Bree to stay in the car, assuring her he would not be long.

Bree thought, *'Hmm … I wonder what he is up to?'*

After completing the paperwork, the duty manager showed Cody directions to the little house that was hidden amongst the trees. It had a big verandah stretching all the way across the front that looked out towards the east.

When they pulled up in front of the house Cody asked Bree to close her eyes.

"Why?" she asked.

"Could you please close your eyes? I have a surprise for you."

So, Bree closed her eyes just as Cody had asked, and then she felt him help her out of the ute. He guided her down to the front door.

"Okay, Bree, open your eyes."

Bree was speechless! Looking in through the open doorway she saw huge vases of red roses, a basket of food, a bottle of champagne, and then she saw rose petals scattered all across the floor.

At first, Bree could not speak, and then she turned to Cody. "Why?" was all she said.

Cody went to her and wrapped his arms around her. Looking into her face, he said, "Bree, I love you. You were nearly taken from me in the accident, and all this is to show you how much you mean to me."

Bree was speechless, she rested against Cody's muscular body, hugging him. She brought her head up and looked into his eyes.

"I don't deserve all this, but thank you … I love it!"

"Oh, there is one more surprise, but that is for later," said Cody mysteriously.

Bree thought, *'How could he top this?'* She had never seen anything so beautiful.

Cody brought in their suitcases while Bree made them a coffee and a sandwich to eat. They sat out on the verandah for hours drinking their coffee and eating their sandwiches while taking in the view.

The sunset here was different to home, but still just as beautiful. The orange rays of the sunset lit up the sky and Bree spotted the evening star. She was feeling relaxed and spoilt, a much different feeling to being on the farm. But she loved it, and she and Cody were together — with no interruptions.

Dinner time was approaching and Cody said, "Um … you did bring a nice dress to wear, didn't you? I have something special planned for tonight."

"Yes, I've brought something nice to wear — just like you asked me to. Cody, this is all too much!"

"No, it's not too much. Why don't you go and get ready for dinner?"

"Okay." Bree hugged Cody, and then she reached up and gave him a kiss on the cheek.

After about an hour Bree came out of the bedroom. She took a sharp breath in as she opened the door.

The whole lounge room and the little walkway leading out onto the verandah was covered in lit candles. Bree could not believe her eyes. *'What is going on?'* she wondered. She had never seen anything so beautiful.

The verandah was decorated with even more glowing candles and a table set for two. Cody was standing at the table in his suit.

Bree thought, *'Oh my, he is so handsome!'*

Cody looked at Bree with approval written all over his face. She looked *so* pretty in soft pink; it was certainly a special dress—perfect for a very special occasion.

Bree walked towards Cody, "What's all this? It's so beautiful! You didn't have to go to all this trouble for me ... but I'm glad you did." She reached up and embraced Cody with a passionate kiss.

At that very moment there was a knock at the door.

'What, even up here we get interrupted?!' thought Bree. Cody went to the front door and two ladies walked into the house carrying large, covered silver trays which they unloaded onto the dining table. Once they had done that they went to the fridge and put some of

the food into it. Then they said goodnight and left.

Dining on the verandah, Cody and Bree enjoyed a delicious meal, and they talked easily about everything and nothing in particular: the scenic view, their busy lives on the farm, laughing about things they both found funny.

After the meal, Cody went inside to get their dessert, while he was inside he made sure he had the ring box in his pocket. Cody took a big breath, *'It's now or never,'* he thought, and he took their desserts outside on to the verandah.

After they finished their dessert, Bree sat back and looked out at the view, there were lights in the distance, but that was all, she could hear nothing; it was so peaceful.

Cody asked Bree if she was alright.

"Yes, thanks, I am. I'm quite full after that amazing meal, and I'm enjoying the peace and quiet."

Cody got up and moved towards Bree, taking her hand he led her to the middle of the verandah.

Bree took in a sharp, quick breath as she watched Cody go down on one knee.

"Brenda Douglas, you are my best friend, my one true love, the person I care more about than anyone else in this world. Will you do me the honour of marrying me?" All the time Cody was holding open the little red box that had the beautiful diamond ring in it.

Bree had tears in her eyes, she opened her mouth to speak, and nothing came out. She swallowed and said, "Yes, Yes, Yes! I will marry you Cody!"

He stood up and saw the tears now falling down Bree's beautiful face. He put the ring on her finger, and it fitted perfectly.

Cody embraced Bree, and they shared a long and passionate kiss. Then he said, "This is why I couldn't tell you anything about this weekend. I wanted it to be special, and for us to be by ourselves: no family, no friends. Just something we can both remember."

Bree looked at him lovingly and said, "How could I ever forget all of this? Yes, it is *so* special, I've never experienced anything like this before. Cody, I've told you that I have strong feelings for you, but I have never said the words. I love you. I think I have for a long time." She allowed her words to sink in, and then she added, "You have always been there for me. Remember back to our camping trip, when I saw Bob? How you looked after me, comforted me, and made sure I was alright? Well, from that day on I started to fall in love with you, but I was frightened of getting hurt again, and you gave me time. Thank you for all of that."

Bree and Cody held each other, enjoying the peace and the feeling of one another in their arms. Then Cody broke the moment by saying, "Oh, I forgot to say, how beautiful you look in that dress. I don't think I've seen you wear it before."

"Olivia and I bought it not long ago when she took me to Braham."

After a moment's silence Cody asked quietly, "You never told me why you went to Braham by yourself that time."

"Um … it was to see a psychologist … to help me with my mental and emotional health after all the trauma of the last year or so. I realised that it was all weighing me down: you know everything I've been through, and then when I thought you and Ashley were back together, well you know …" she replied slowly.

"Are you okay, Bree? Is everything alright?" Cody was genuinely worried.

"The psychologist says I am recovering well, but I still need to check in with her regularly. Please don't say anything to anyone about it, I just want to get on with living my life."

"Thanks for sharing that with me, it's great that you're getting the help you need, and you know you can trust me with anything," Cody said softly. He then poured a glass of champagne for Bree and one for himself.

In between sips Bree said, "A while ago you said it was up to me if I was ready for us to make love."

Cody looked at Bree, his heart thumping.

Bree took their glasses of champagne and put them both on the table. She kissed Cody passionately again.

"I'm ready. Take me to bed, Cody.

* * *

The next morning, Bree awoke to a loving kiss, and a steaming mug of coffee.

"Morning, Mrs. Patrick to-be!" said Cody. Bree smiled and reached up to Cody and kissed him back.

Bree admired the full length of Cody's powerful physique; naked from the waist up, his tanned chest and his muscular body all accentuated in the morning sunlight. It reminded her of the previous night, and she felt a warm glow all over her. Cody moved onto the bed and wrapped his arms around her.

"I'm not being rude, but what do you think my mum and dad, and your dad will say about this?"

"Well, they all knew I had this weekend planned. They were happy about it all. I spoke to your dad earlier this week and I asked him for your hand in marriage, so I did have your mum's and dad's blessings."

Bree turned to look at Cody, "What did Dad say?"

Cody smiled and did his best impression of Paul, "My goodness, boy, it's taken you so long to get around to it. I dread to think how long I will have to wait for a grandchild! You have my blessing, and Beth's too. Look after my girl, please, Cody."

"Dad said that about a grandchild. Oh my goodness!" Then, looking directly at Cody, Bree said, "Kids are something we've never talked about."

"I'd like four to six kids," said Cody, grinning.

Bree laughed, "Me … more like two to four kids, but we will see, okay? Deal!"

"I don't care, as long as they are healthy, and the girls are as beautiful as you."

"Hmm … do you think we should ring my mum and dad, and your dad too?"

"I think so, it will make their day."

Cody put on a white singlet and Bree slipped her black satin nightie on, then she phoned home and Beth answered. Bree said, "Hi Mum, how are you and Dad?" When Beth said they were both fine, Bree continued, "Mum we have some news. Is Dad near to the phone?

"Paul, get over here quick!" ordered Beth.

"Hi, girl," Paul said into the handpiece while holding it for the two of them.

Cody said, "Hi, Mum and Dad, we're ringing you to let you both know that we're engaged."

Paul handed the phone back to Beth and danced around the kitchen yelling out, "Yippee! Yippee!"

Cody and Bree could only laugh. It would have been a sight to see Paul dancing.

Beth said, "Congratulations you two, we love you both!" And then before ending the call she added, "You should phone Thomas now."

Cody phoned his dad immediately after ending the call to Beth, but he made it a video call so Thomas could see them both.

"Hi, Dad. How are you?" said Cody.

"Hi, son, I'm well. How are both of you? I have to say you both look incredibly happy."

"Dad, we have some news. We're engaged." And with that, Bree brought up her left hand for Thomas to see the engagement ring.

"Boy, son, you have done well with the ring!" Thomas said. "Congratulations to both of you. Bree, have you told your mum and dad?"

"Yes, Thomas, we just rang Mum and Dad to let them know," said Bree.

Thomas said, smiling, "It's not Thomas anymore, its Dad." They said their goodbyes and ended the call.

Bree then said to Cody, "How about we take a picture, just for *our* memories?"

"Yep, great idea," affirmed Cody.

Cody cuddled Bree, and Bree put her left hand up on Cody's chest so the engagement ring could be seen in the selfie. They would treasure the photo of this moment for the rest of their lives.

Bree looked lovingly into Cody's eyes and said, "I love you, Cody Patrick!"

Then she rolled over on top of Cody and gave him a passionate kiss. And they began again from where they had left off the night before …

EPILOGUE

Bree and Cody arrived home on Sunday around lunchtime after their romantic weekend away. Cody had rung ahead and asked his dad, Thomas, to be over at The Flats when they got back.

When they arrived Beth, Paul, and Thomas came out to meet them. Hugs all around for Bree and Cody, and then Thomas helped Cody inside with their suitcases.

"Show us the ring!" said Beth excitedly.

"Bree, you're going to have to look after this ring, especially one this size," suggested Thomas. Then he whispered to Cody, "Have you insured the ring?" Cody quietly answered that he had already insured it as it was quite an expensive piece of jewellery.

Cody and Bree asked everyone not to say a word as they were going to tell everyone else at the barbecue they had arranged for Saturday night.

"It's a celebration of my birthday and Cody's birthday, but what the others don't know is it's also to celebrate our engagement," explained Bree.

Thomas spoke up, "Paul, Beth, I'm going to pay for it all," he continued, "I'll organise all of my workers and my cook to come over and do everything, and I'll phone the bottle shop in Braham—the owners are friends of mine—and I'll order all the drinks."

Paul thanked Thomas for his kindness, and then turned to Cody and Bree and asked, "Who have you both invited?"

Cody replied, "All the blokes and their girlfriends, Phil, Johnno and Jenny, and Ruth from the grocery store." He then turned to his dad and asked, "Dad, would you contact Pat Conroy and invite him up for the barbecue too?"

* * *

On Friday Thomas's workers came over and set up everything for the party. They put up the marquee and decorated it all around with twinkling fairy lights, and then they strung more lights to the house and the fence, and even in the big tree in the back yard. Beth, Paul, Cody, and Bree couldn't believe how much trouble Thomas was going to for the party.

* * *

Late on Saturday afternoon Bree got ready for the barbecue; she had a shower, and the cool water felt refreshing as the weather was so hot. She decided to wear the dress she wore when Cody asked her to marry him.

Everyone started to arrive at around 6 p.m. Thomas greeted everyone and showed them where the bar was, and told them to have fun. The party was in full swing, when Thomas and Paul got up and each gave a short speech, wishing Bree and Cody the happiest of birthdays.

Then Cody and Bree thanked everyone for coming out and celebrating their birthdays, particularly after the year they both had experienced. The Patricks' cook brought out two birthday cakes and Bree and Cody blew out the candles. Then Cody reached for Bree's hand and winked at her.

"Some of you know I took Bree away last weekend for her birthday. While we were away I asked her a question … and she said *Yes!*"

With that Cody raised Bree's hand up showing everyone the engagement ring. There was clapping from everyone, and Nick, Rick, and Paul all let out a 'Yippeeeee!'

The cook brought out another cake, and this time he had put a bride and groom decoration on the top of the cake, which brought laughter from everyone.

Paul said to Thomas, "Well, the wedding is the next thing. Just hope I don't have to wait as long for that as I did for Cody to ask Bree to marry him."

Thomas laughed, "Yep, you are so right there, Paul."

Nick leaned in to Olivia and said, "Well, Cody

definitely isn't the 'fifth wheel' anymore."

Olivia smiled and turned to BJ and said, "Looks like you're next, BJ."

BJ laughed, and said "Yep, I just have to find a woman like Bree!"

About the Author

BIANCA TODD

In her book, *Love After Dutchman's Road,* Bianca explores themes from her own life experience, particularly living and working in rural Australia, and weaves them into a charming, authentic and heart-warming romantic story.

Bianca chooses to live a quiet life in Queensland, Australia, where she writes for the enjoyment of others.

Acknowledgements

Deborah Fay at Disruptive Publishing, thank you for all your help, advice, and wisdom in getting my book published. Thank you for believing in me, even when I didn't.

Words cannot adequately express my gratitude, my admiration, and my thanks to Jo Scott for her patience, advice, and assistance in editing my first manuscript. The guidance, the feedback sessions, and all the moral support she has given me throughout editing my book has been invaluable.

Jo's expertise has made my life so much easier as an author, and she has taught me so much through the process. Again thank you for working your magic. I would highly recommend Jo to any author.

What's next

Bianca continues to write fiction and she is presently working on a series of novels following on from *Love After Dutchman's Road* set in the beautiful Australian landscape she knows so well.

Expect to see more from Bianca Todd.